SCRIPT ADAPTATION
Didier Le Bornec

PENCILS
Mario Cortes

INK
Comicup Studio

ABDOBOOKS.COM

Reinforced library bound edition published in 2021 by Spotlight, a division of ABDO, PO Box 398166, Minneapolis, Minnesota 55439. Spotlight produces high-quality reinforced library bound editions for schools and libraries. Published by agreement with Disney Enterprises, Inc.

Printed in the United States of America, North Mankato, Minnesota.
042020
092020

THIS BOOK CONTAINS RECYCLED MATERIALS

The Aristocats is based on the book by Thomas Rowe.

Library of Congress Control Number: 2020933049

Publisher's Cataloging-in-Publication Data

Names: Le Bornec, Didier, author. | Cortes, Mario, illustrator.
Title: The Aristocats / by Didier Le Bornec; illustrated by Mario Cortes.
Description: Minneapolis, Minnesota: Spotlight, 2021. | Series: Disney classics
Summary: When their owner says she wants to leave her fortune to her cats, the jealous butler leaves the family of felines in the country, and they must find their way home with the help of a smooth talking tomcat.
Identifiers: ISBN 9781532145322 (lib. bdg.)
Subjects: LCSH: Aristocats (Motion picture)--Juvenile fiction. | Cats--Juvenile fiction. | France--Paris--Juvenile fiction. | Inheritance and succession--Juvenile fiction. | Butlers--Juvenile fiction. | Adventure Stories--Juvenile fiction. | Graphic novels--Juvenile fiction.
Classification: DDC 741.5--dc23

ABDO
Spotlight

A Division of ABDO
abdobooks.com

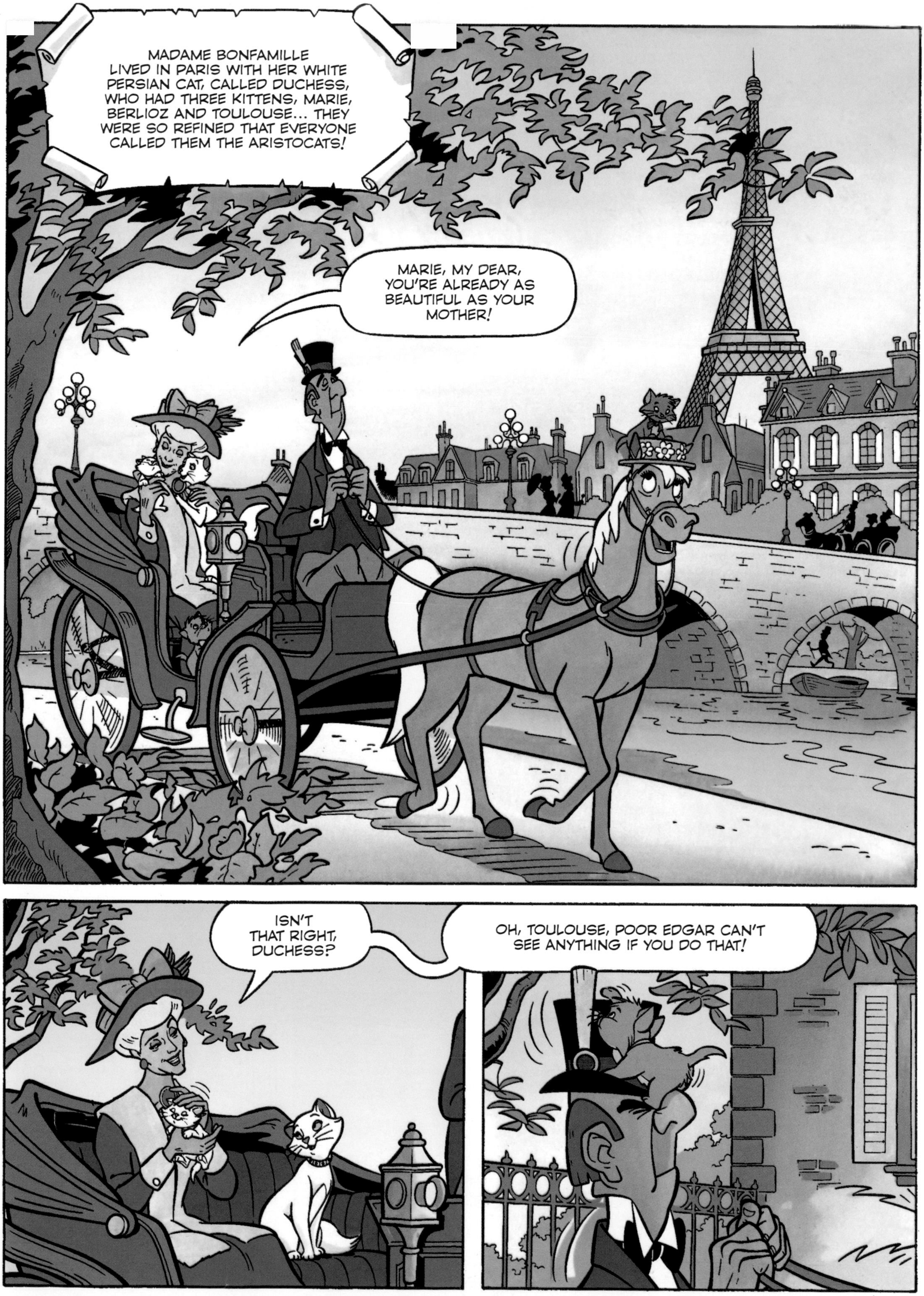
MADAME BONFAMILLE LIVED IN PARIS WITH HER WHITE PERSIAN CAT, CALLED DUCHESS, WHO HAD THREE KITTENS, MARIE, BERLIOZ AND TOULOUSE... THEY WERE SO REFINED THAT EVERYONE CALLED THEM THE ARISTOCATS!
MARIE, MY DEAR, YOU'RE ALREADY AS BEAUTIFUL AS YOUR MOTHER!
ISN'T THAT RIGHT, DUCHESS?
OH, TOULOUSE, POOR EDGAR CAN'T SEE ANYTHING IF YOU DO THAT!

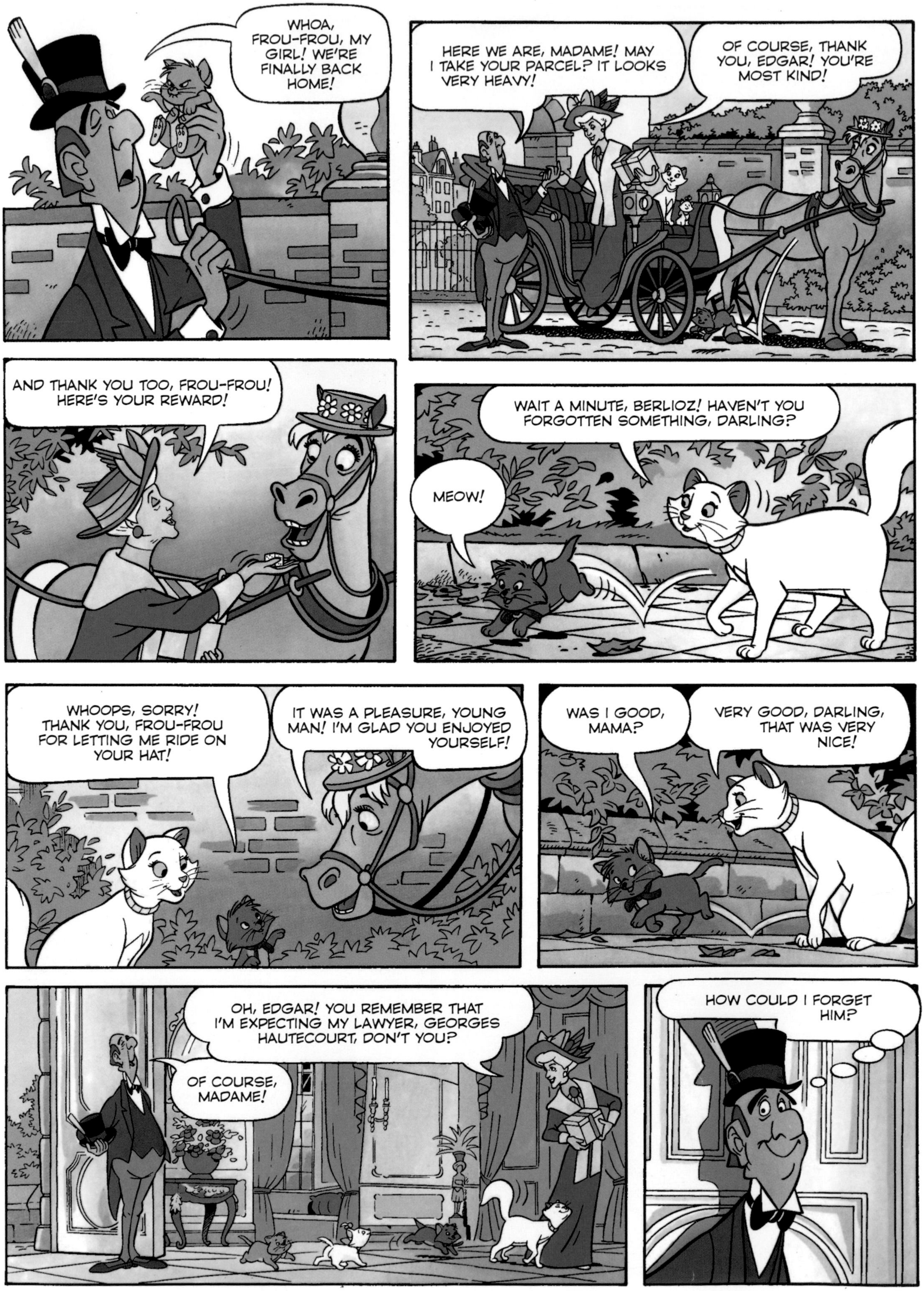
WHOA, FROU-FROU, MY GIRL! WE'RE FINALLY BACK HOME!
HERE WE ARE, MADAME! MAY I TAKE YOUR PARCEL? IT LOOKS VERY HEAVY!
OF COURSE, THANK YOU, EDGAR! YOU'RE MOST KIND!
AND THANK YOU TOO, FROU-FROU! HERE'S YOUR REWARD!
WAIT A MINUTE, BERLIOZ! HAVEN'T YOU FORGOTTEN SOMETHING, DARLING?
MEOW!
WHOOPS, SORRY! THANK YOU, FROU-FROU FOR LETTING ME RIDE ON YOUR HAT!
IT WAS A PLEASURE, YOUNG MAN! I'M GLAD YOU ENJOYED YOURSELF!
WAS I GOOD, MAMA?
VERY GOOD, DARLING, THAT WAS VERY NICE!
OH, EDGAR! YOU REMEMBER THAT I'M EXPECTING MY LAWYER, GEORGES HAUTECOURT, DON'T YOU?
OF COURSE, MADAME!
HOW COULD I FORGET HIM?

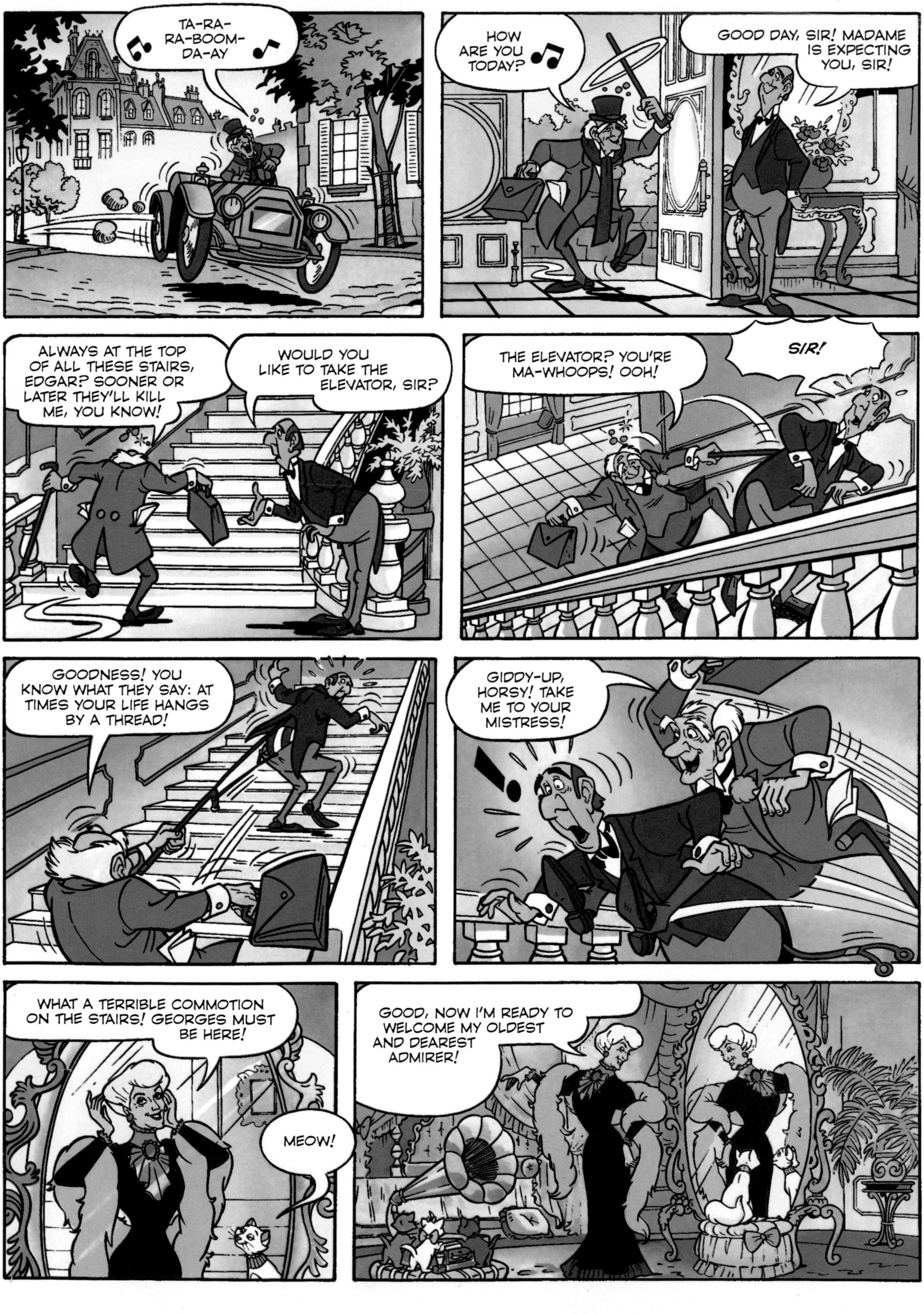
TA-RA-RA-BOOM-DA-AY
HOW ARE YOU TODAY?
GOOD DAY, SIR! MADAME IS EXPECTING YOU, SIR!
ALWAYS AT THE TOP OF ALL THESE STAIRS, EDGAR? SOONER OR LATER THEY'LL KILL ME, YOU KNOW!
WOULD YOU LIKE TO TAKE THE ELEVATOR, SIR?
THE ELEVATOR? YOU'RE MA-WHOOPS! OOH!
SIR!
GOODNESS! YOU KNOW WHAT THEY SAY: AT TIMES YOUR LIFE HANGS BY A THREAD!
GIDDY-UP, HORSY! TAKE ME TO YOUR MISTRESS!
WHAT A TERRIBLE COMMOTION ON THE STAIRS! GEORGES MUST BE HERE!
MEOW!
GOOD, NOW I'M READY TO WELCOME MY OLDEST AND DEAREST ADMIRER!

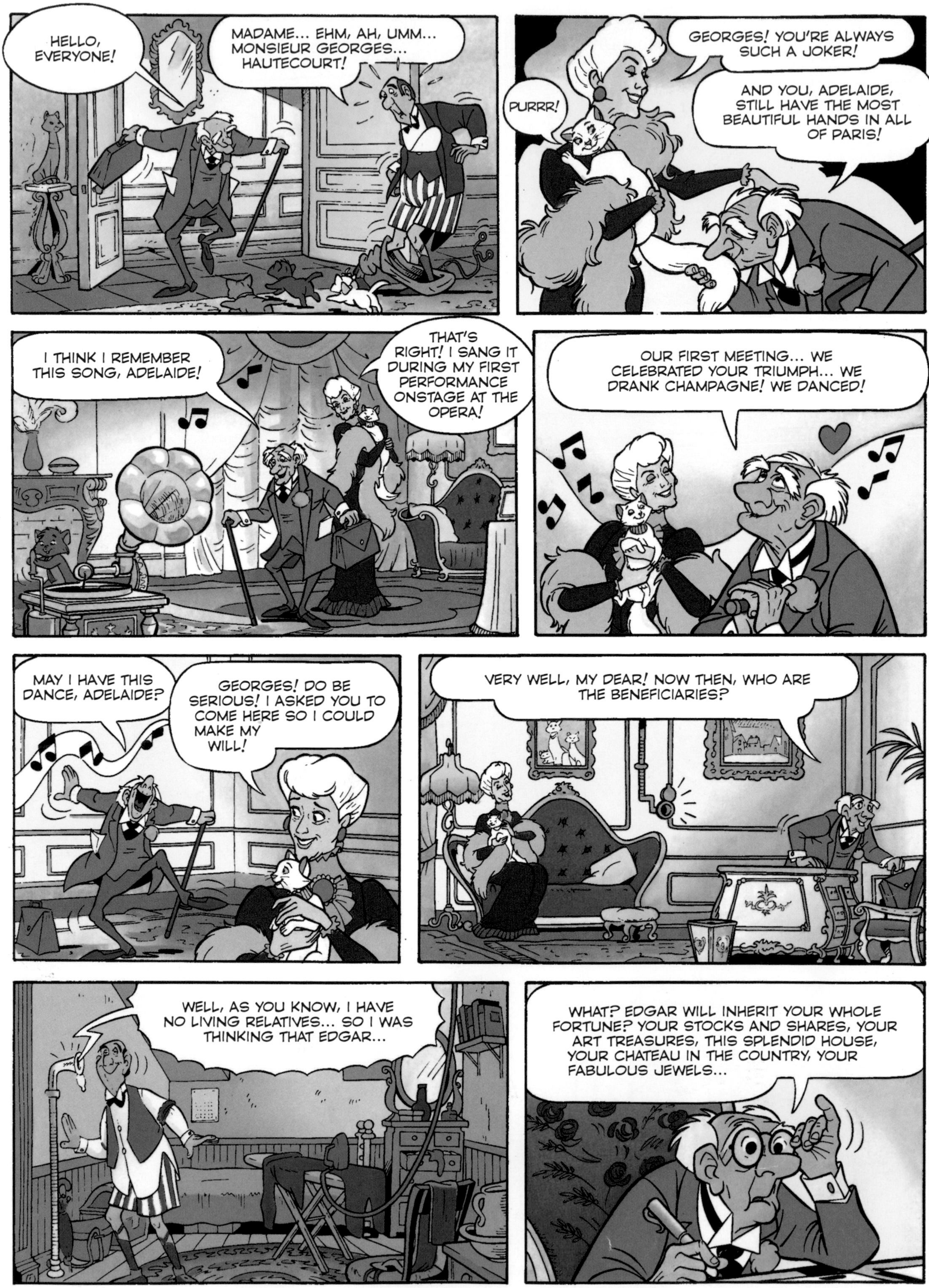
HELLO, EVERYONE!
MADAME... EHM, AH, UMM... MONSIEUR GEORGES... HAUTECOURT!
PURRR!
GEORGES! YOU'RE ALWAYS SUCH A JOKER!
AND YOU, ADELAIDE, STILL HAVE THE MOST BEAUTIFUL HANDS IN ALL OF PARIS!
I THINK I REMEMBER THIS SONG, ADELAIDE!
THAT'S RIGHT! I SANG IT DURING MY FIRST PERFORMANCE ONSTAGE AT THE OPERA!
OUR FIRST MEETING... WE CELEBRATED YOUR TRIUMPH... WE DRANK CHAMPAGNE! WE DANCED!
MAY I HAVE THIS DANCE, ADELAIDE?
GEORGES! DO BE SERIOUS! I ASKED YOU TO COME HERE SO I COULD MAKE MY WILL!
VERY WELL, MY DEAR! NOW THEN, WHO ARE THE BENEFICIARIES?
WELL, AS YOU KNOW, I HAVE NO LIVING RELATIVES... SO I WAS THINKING THAT EDGAR...
WHAT? EDGAR WILL INHERIT YOUR WHOLE FORTUNE? YOUR STOCKS AND SHARES, YOUR ART TREASURES, THIS SPLENDID HOUSE, YOUR CHATEAU IN THE COUNTRY, YOUR FABULOUS JEWELS...

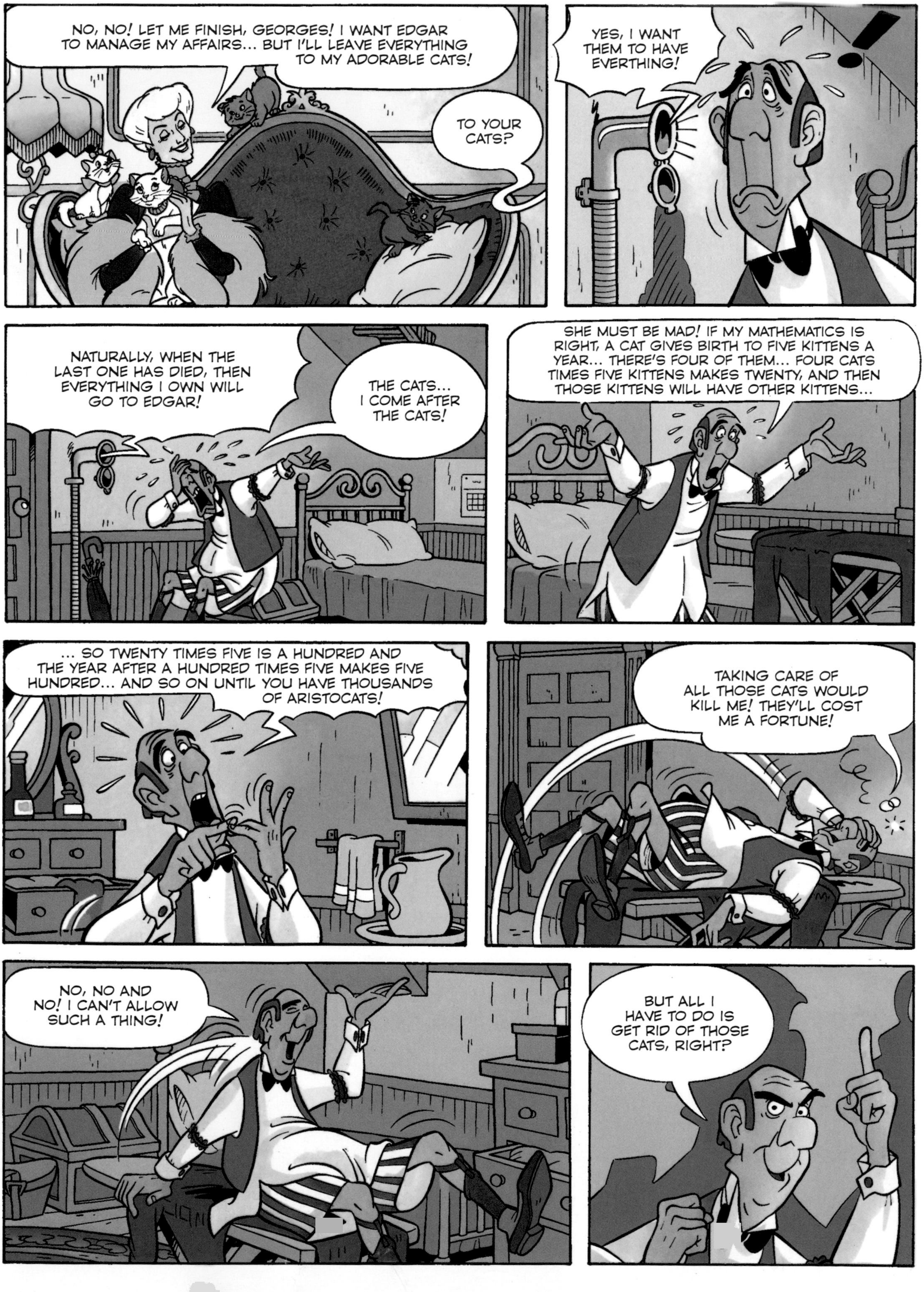
NO, NO! LET ME FINISH, GEORGES! I WANT EDGAR TO MANAGE MY AFFAIRS... BUT I'LL LEAVE EVERYTHING TO MY ADORABLE CATS!
TO YOUR CATS?
YES, I WANT THEM TO HAVE EVERTHING!
NATURALLY, WHEN THE LAST ONE HAS DIED, THEN EVERYTHING I OWN WILL GO TO EDGAR!
THE CATS... I COME AFTER THE CATS!
SHE MUST BE MAD! IF MY MATHEMATICS IS RIGHT, A CAT GIVES BIRTH TO FIVE KITTENS A YEAR... THERE'S FOUR OF THEM... FOUR CATS TIMES FIVE KITTENS MAKES TWENTY, AND THEN THOSE KITTENS WILL HAVE OTHER KITTENS...
... SO TWENTY TIMES FIVE IS A HUNDRED AND THE YEAR AFTER A HUNDRED TIMES FIVE MAKES FIVE HUNDRED... AND SO ON UNTIL YOU HAVE THOUSANDS OF ARISTOCATS!
TAKING CARE OF ALL THOSE CATS WOULD KILL ME! THEY'LL COST ME A FORTUNE!
NO, NO AND NO! I CAN'T ALLOW SUCH A THING!
BUT ALL I HAVE TO DO IS GET RID OF THOSE CATS, RIGHT?

LATER THE SAME EVENING...

MARIE! STOP IT! THAT'S NOT HOW A LADY SHOULD BEHAVE!

TAKE THAT! AND THAT! MAMA! OW!

IT WASN'T MY FAULT, MAMA! BERLIOZ SCRATCHED ME AND BIT MY EAR!

BERLIOZ! A GENTLEMAN SHOULDN'T SCRATCH A LADY OR BITE HER EAR!

AND HOW AM I GOING TO LEARN HOW TO DEFEND MYSELF IN CASE I MEET A TOUGH ALLEY CAT?

OH, WHAT A TERRIBLE THOUGHT! NOW COME HERE AND LEARN SOMETHING MORE APPROPRIATE BEFORE DINNER!

MARIE! BERLIOZ! CONTINUE WITH YOUR PIANO EXERCISES! TOULOUSE, PAINT SOMETHING!

ALRIGHT, MAMA!

LOOK, I'M AS GOOD AS TOULOUSE-LAUTREC!

OH, BUT THAT'S DEAR EDGAR!

EXACTLY! THAT'S THE OLD RATFACE!

RATFACE! THAT'S FUNNY!

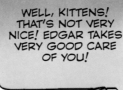

WELL, KITTENS! THAT'S NOT VERY NICE! EDGAR TAKES VERY GOOD CARE OF YOU!

I'LL JUST PUT A FEW SLEEPING PILLS IN THEIR MILK AND THOSE FOUR-LEGGED DEMONS WILL BE FAR FROM HERE WHEN THEY WAKE UP AGAIN! HA! HA! HA!

A LITTLE LATER...

DOE ME SO ME DOE ME SO ME FA LA SO IT GOES... WHEN YOU SING YOUR SCALES AND YOUR ARPEGGIOS...

GOOD, MARIE! AND YOU TOO, BERLIOZ! YOU PLAY BEAUTIFULLY!

DOE ME SO ME DOE ME SO ME FA LA...

WHOOPEE!

AHEM! OUR LITTLE DARLINGS' DINNER IS SERVED!

YOUR FAVORITE DISH, CHICKEN SUPREME À LA EDGAR! SWEET DREAMS!

MEOW!

WHOOPS... I MEANT BON APPETIT!

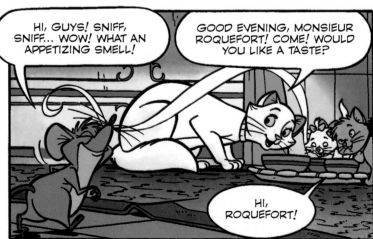

HI, GUYS! SNIFF, SNIFF... WOW! WHAT AN APPETIZING SMELL!

GOOD EVENING, MONSIEUR ROQUEFORT! COME! WOULD YOU LIKE A TASTE?

HI, ROQUEFORT!

WOW... EXQUISITE!

YAWN!

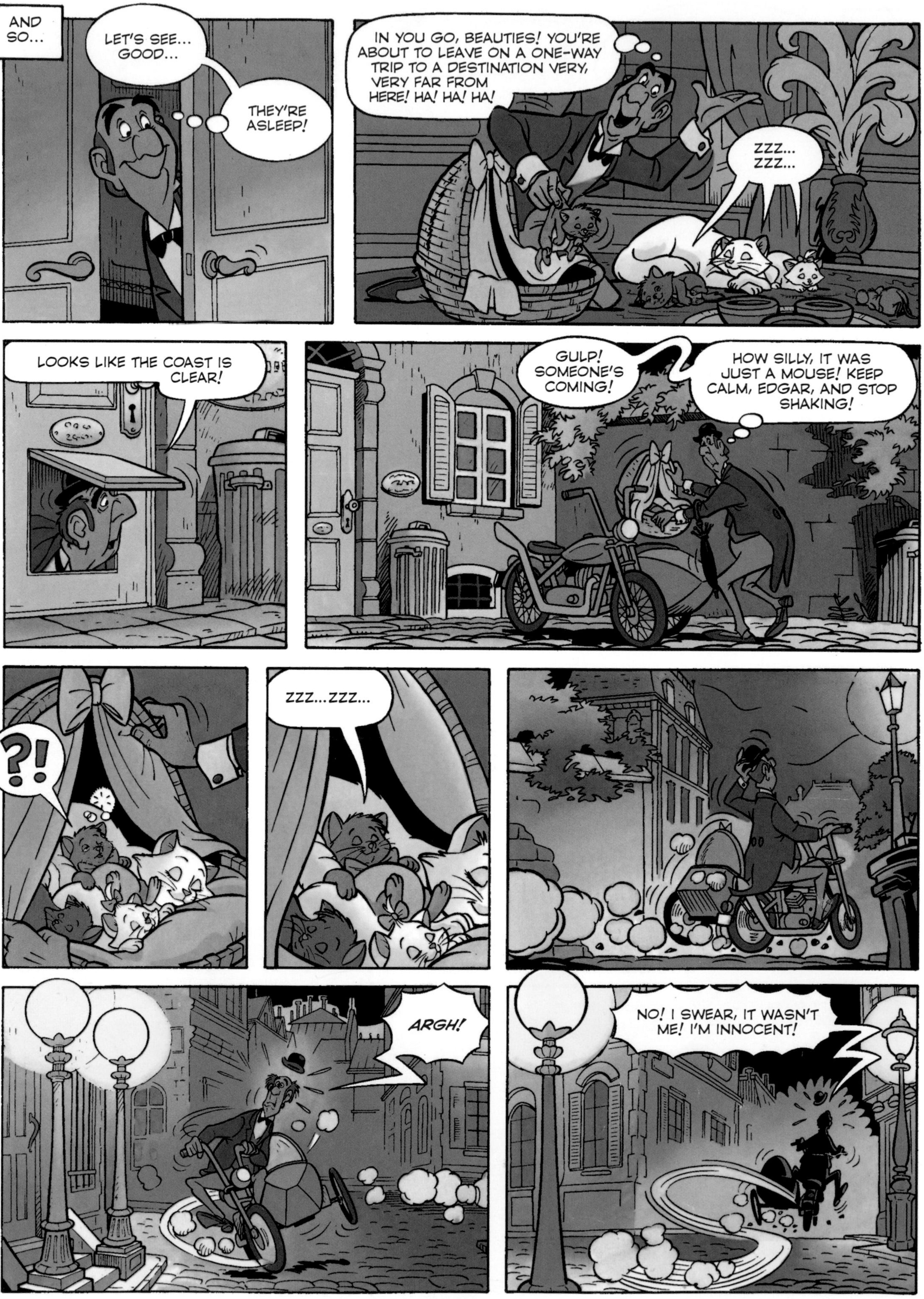
AND SO...
LET'S SEE... GOOD...
THEY'RE ASLEEP!
IN YOU GO, BEAUTIES! YOU'RE ABOUT TO LEAVE ON A ONE-WAY TRIP TO A DESTINATION VERY, VERY FAR FROM HERE! HA! HA! HA!
ZZZ... ZZZ...
LOOKS LIKE THE COAST IS CLEAR!
GULP! SOMEONE'S COMING!
HOW SILLY, IT WAS JUST A MOUSE! KEEP CALM, EDGAR, AND STOP SHAKING!
?!
ZZZ...ZZZ...
ARGH!
NO! I SWEAR, IT WASN'T ME! I'M INNOCENT!

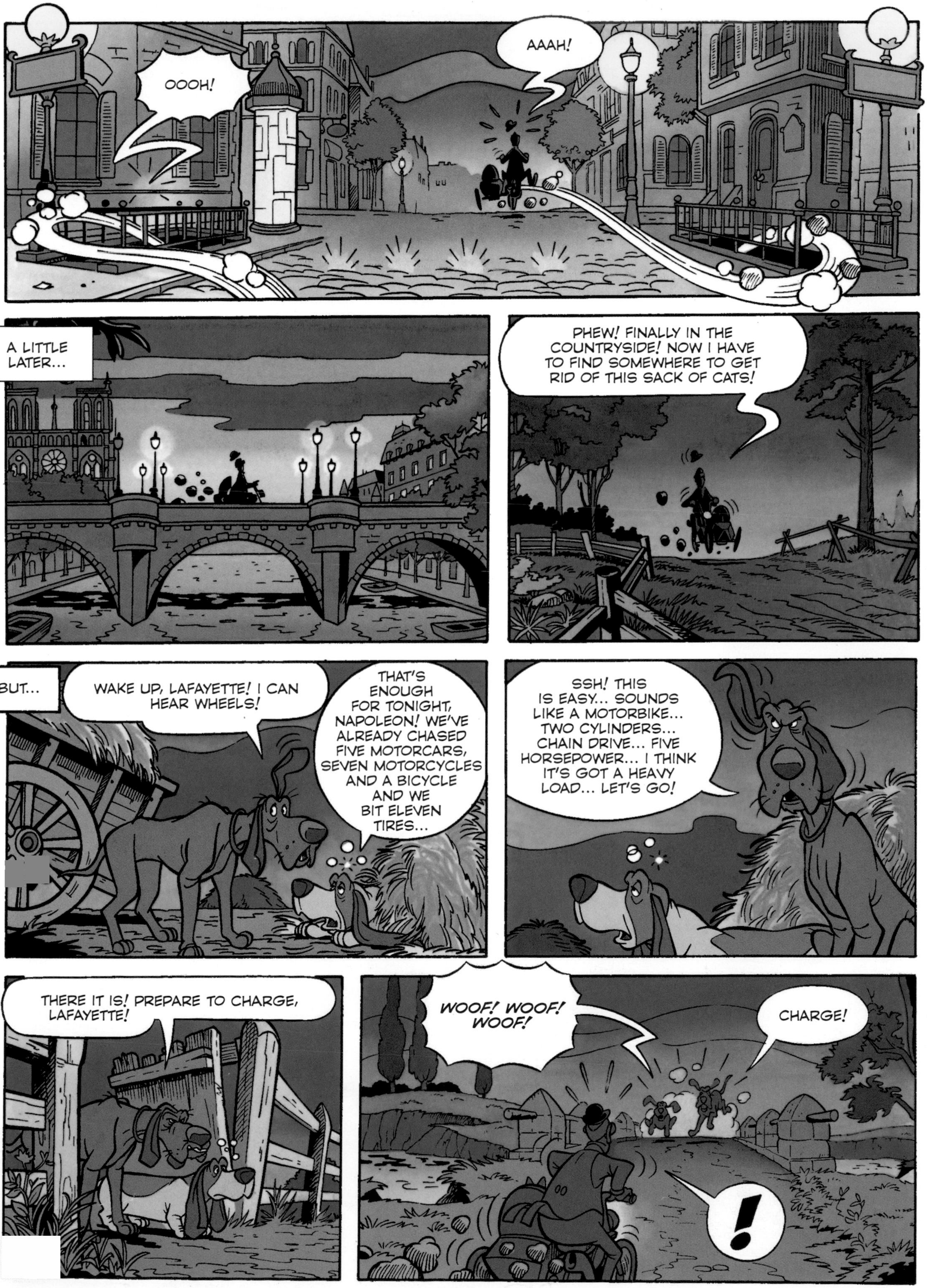
OOOH!
AAAH!
A LITTLE LATER...
PHEW! FINALLY IN THE COUNTRYSIDE! NOW I HAVE TO FIND SOMEWHERE TO GET RID OF THIS SACK OF CATS!
BUT...
WAKE UP, LAFAYETTE! I CAN HEAR WHEELS!
THAT'S ENOUGH FOR TONIGHT, NAPOLEON! WE'VE ALREADY CHASED FIVE MOTORCARS, SEVEN MOTORCYCLES AND A BICYCLE AND WE BIT ELEVEN TIRES...
SSH! THIS IS EASY... SOUNDS LIKE A MOTORBIKE... TWO CYLINDERS... CHAIN DRIVE... FIVE HORSEPOWER... I THINK IT'S GOT A HEAVY LOAD... LET'S GO!
THERE IT IS! PREPARE TO CHARGE, LAFAYETTE!
WOOF! WOOF! WOOF!
CHARGE!
!

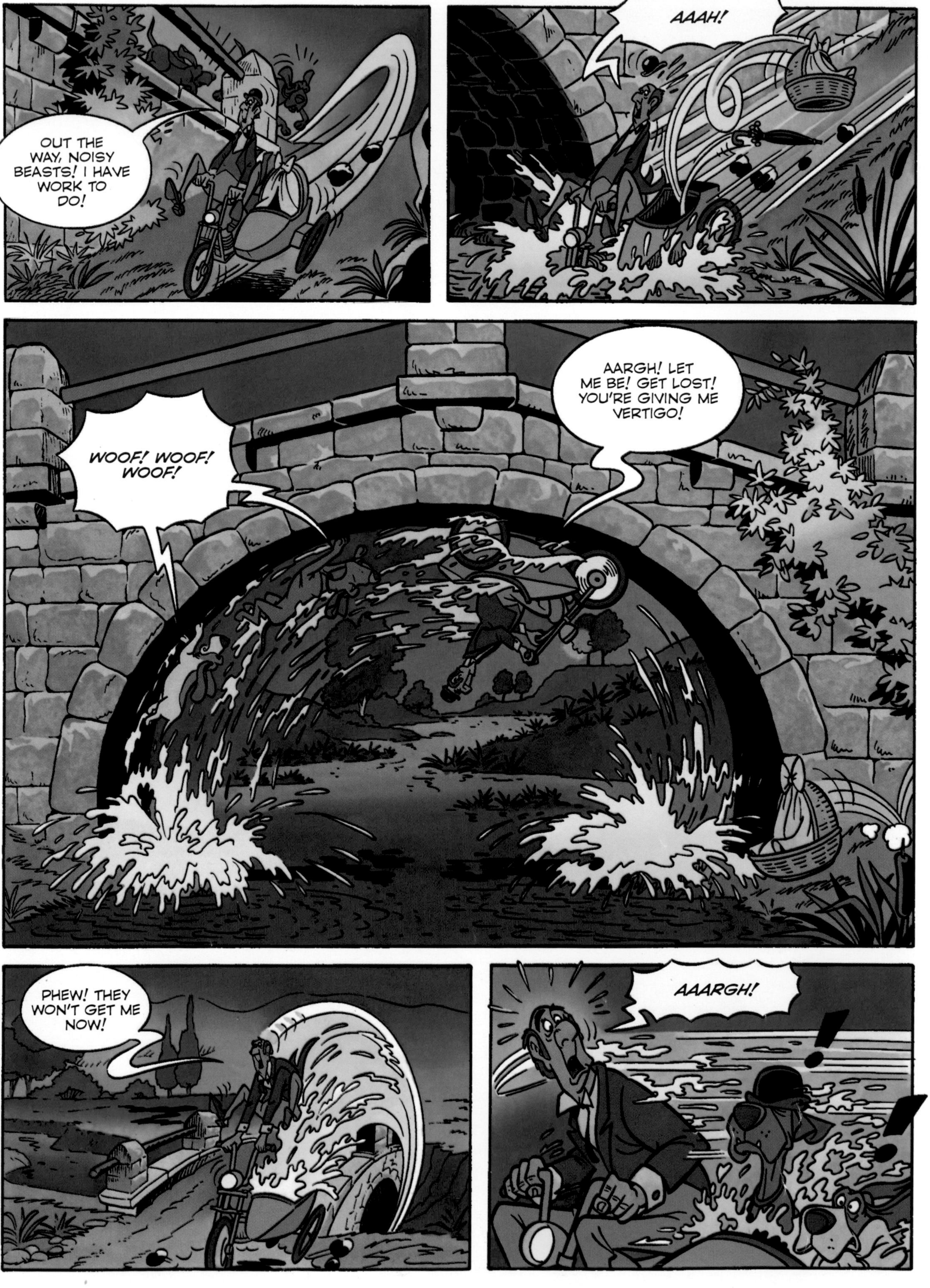
OUT THE WAY, NOISY BEASTS! I HAVE WORK TO DO!
AAAH!
WOOF! WOOF! WOOF!
AARGH! LET ME BE! GET LOST! YOU'RE GIVING ME VERTIGO!
PHEW! THEY WON'T GET ME NOW!
AAARGH!

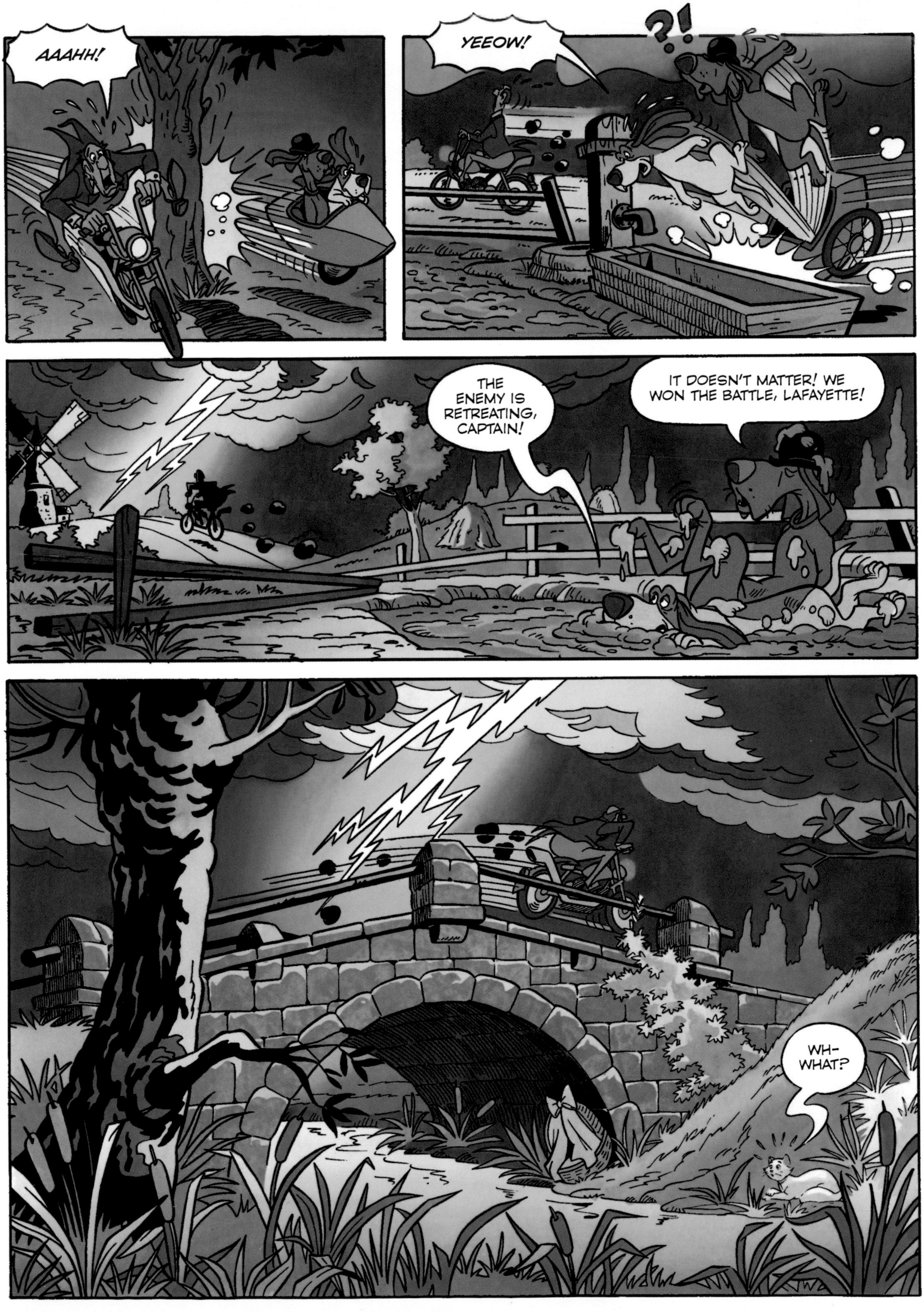
AAAHH!
YEEOW!
?!
THE ENEMY IS RETREATING, CAPTAIN!
IT DOESN'T MATTER! WE WON THE BATTLE, LAFAYETTE!
WH- WHAT?

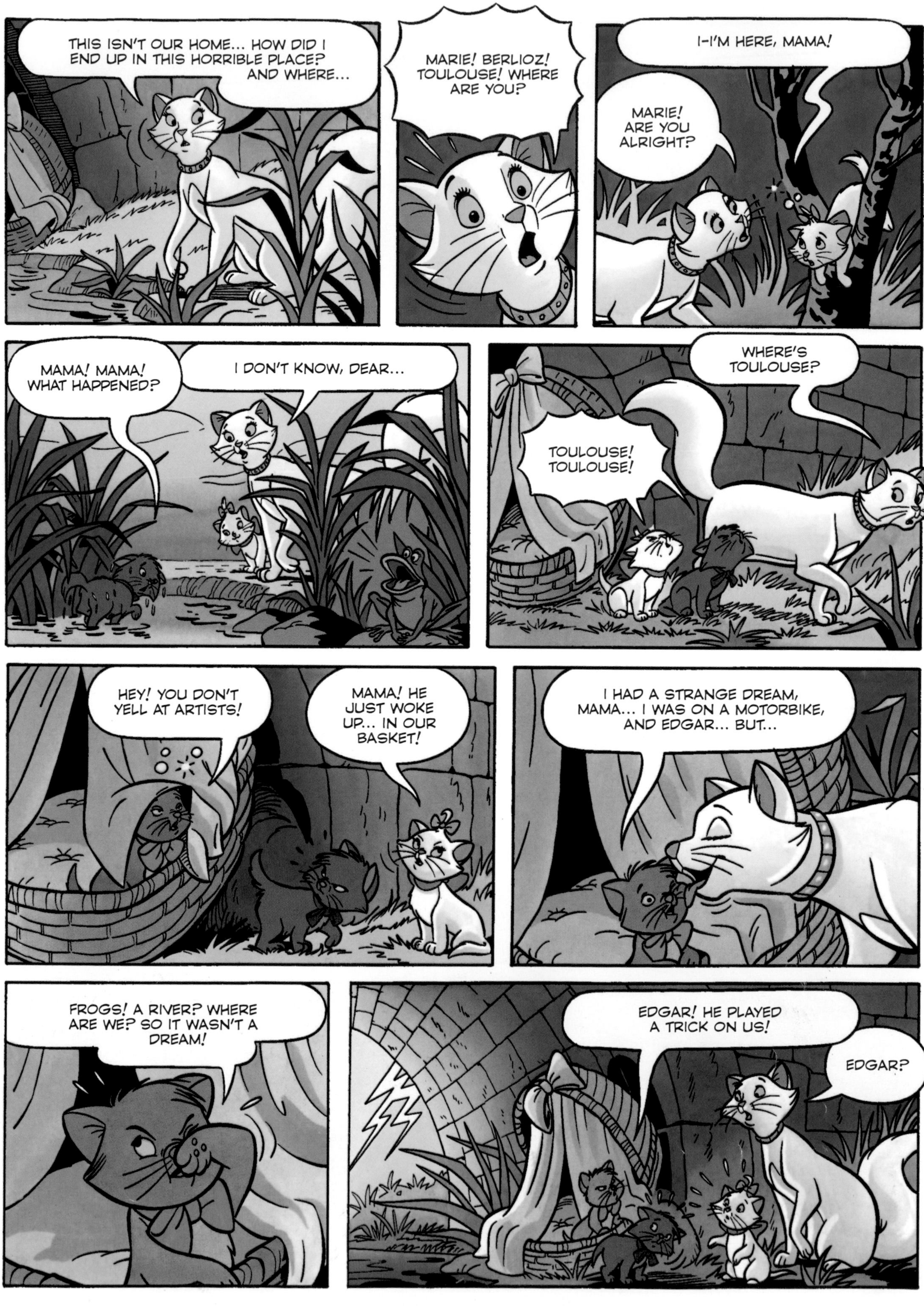
THIS ISN'T OUR HOME... HOW DID I END UP IN THIS HORRIBLE PLACE? AND WHERE...
MARIE! BERLIOZ! TOULOUSE! WHERE ARE YOU?
I-I'M HERE, MAMA!
MARIE! ARE YOU ALRIGHT?
MAMA! MAMA! WHAT HAPPENED?
I DON'T KNOW, DEAR...
WHERE'S TOULOUSE?
TOULOUSE! TOULOUSE!
HEY! YOU DON'T YELL AT ARTISTS!
MAMA! HE JUST WOKE UP... IN OUR BASKET!
I HAD A STRANGE DREAM, MAMA... I WAS ON A MOTORBIKE, AND EDGAR... BUT...
FROGS! A RIVER? WHERE ARE WE? SO IT WASN'T A DREAM!
EDGAR! HE PLAYED A TRICK ON US!
EDGAR?

SUCH A KIND MAN WOULD NEVER HAVE DONE SOMETHING LIKE THIS!

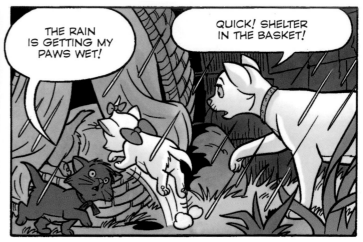

THE RAIN IS GETTING MY PAWS WET!

QUICK! SHELTER IN THE BASKET!

WHAT WILL HAPPEN TO US, MAMA?

I WISH I KNEW, MY DARLINGS! IT DOES LOOK HOPELESS, DOESN'T IT!

I WISH WE WERE HOME WITH MADAME!

POOR MADAME! SHE'LL BE SO WORRIED WHEN SHE FINDS US GONE!

DUCHESS?! KITTENS?!

OH, MY DEARS! I HAD A TERRIBLE DREAM ABOUT YOU!

OH, NO! MY DARLINGS ARE GONE!

DUCHESS! KITTENS!

ZZZ... EH?! WHAT?!

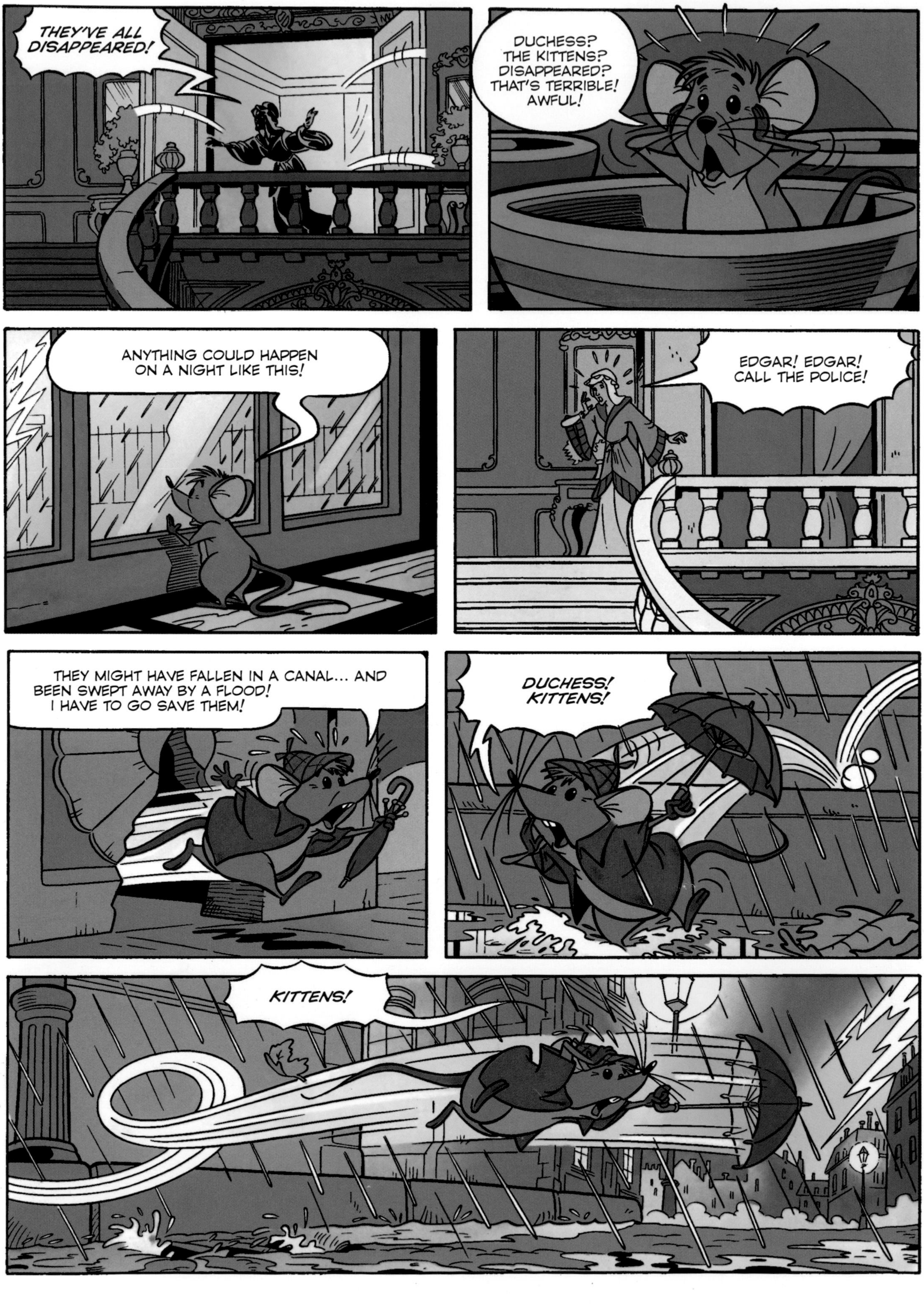
THEY'VE ALL DISAPPEARED!
DUCHESS? THE KITTENS? DISAPPEARED? THAT'S TERRIBLE! AWFUL!
ANYTHING COULD HAPPEN ON A NIGHT LIKE THIS!
EDGAR! EDGAR! CALL THE POLICE!
THEY MIGHT HAVE FALLEN IN A CANAL... AND BEEN SWEPT AWAY BY A FLOOD! I HAVE TO GO SAVE THEM!
DUCHESS! KITTENS!
KITTENS!

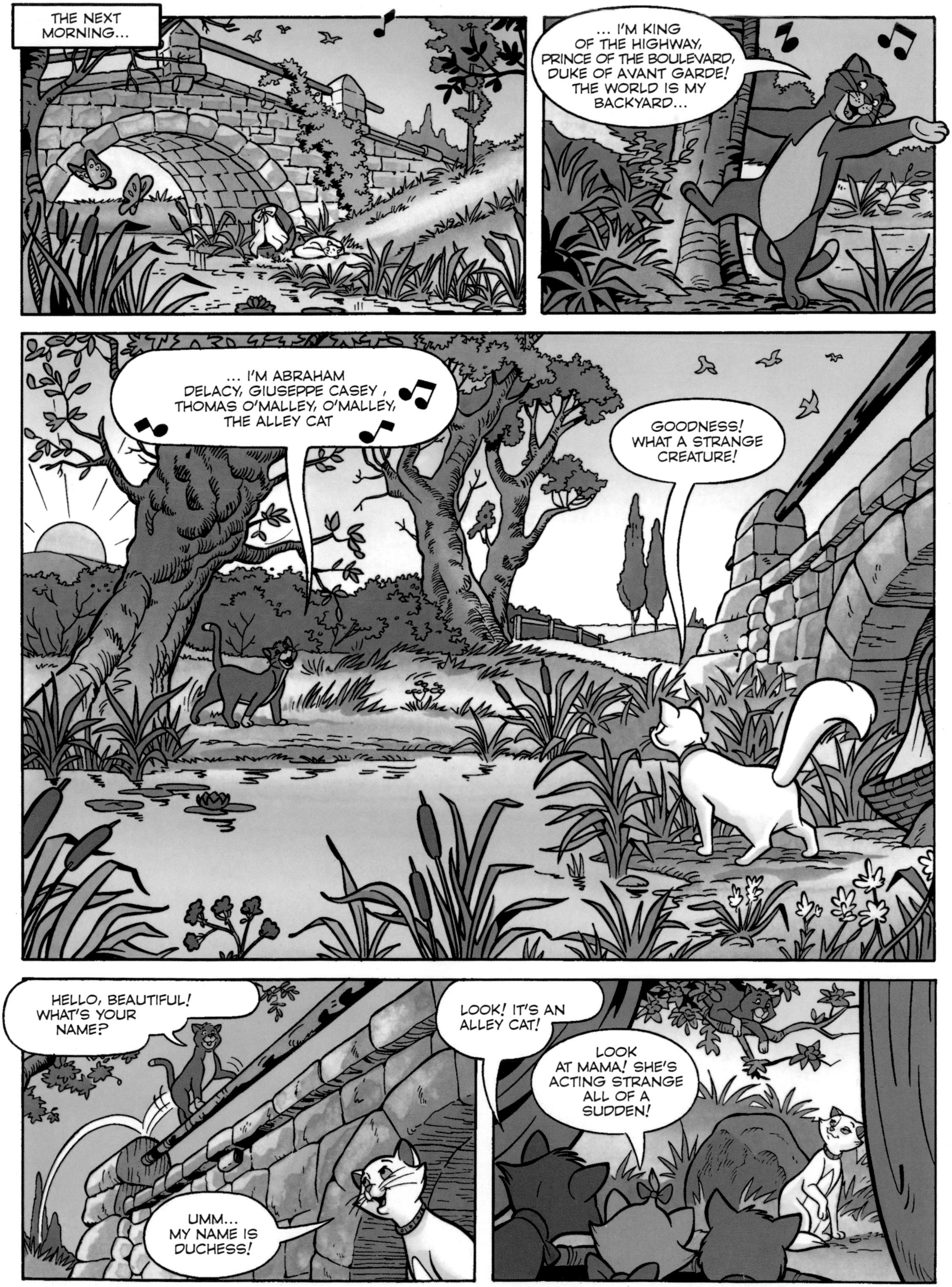
THE NEXT MORNING...
... I'M KING OF THE HIGHWAY, PRINCE OF THE BOULEVARD, DUKE OF AVANT GARDE! THE WORLD IS MY BACKYARD...
... I'M ABRAHAM DELACY, GIUSEPPE CASEY , THOMAS O'MALLEY, O'MALLEY, THE ALLEY CAT
GOODNESS! WHAT A STRANGE CREATURE!
HELLO, BEAUTIFUL! WHAT'S YOUR NAME?
UMM... MY NAME IS DUCHESS!
LOOK! IT'S AN ALLEY CAT!
LOOK AT MAMA! SHE'S ACTING STRANGE ALL OF A SUDDEN!

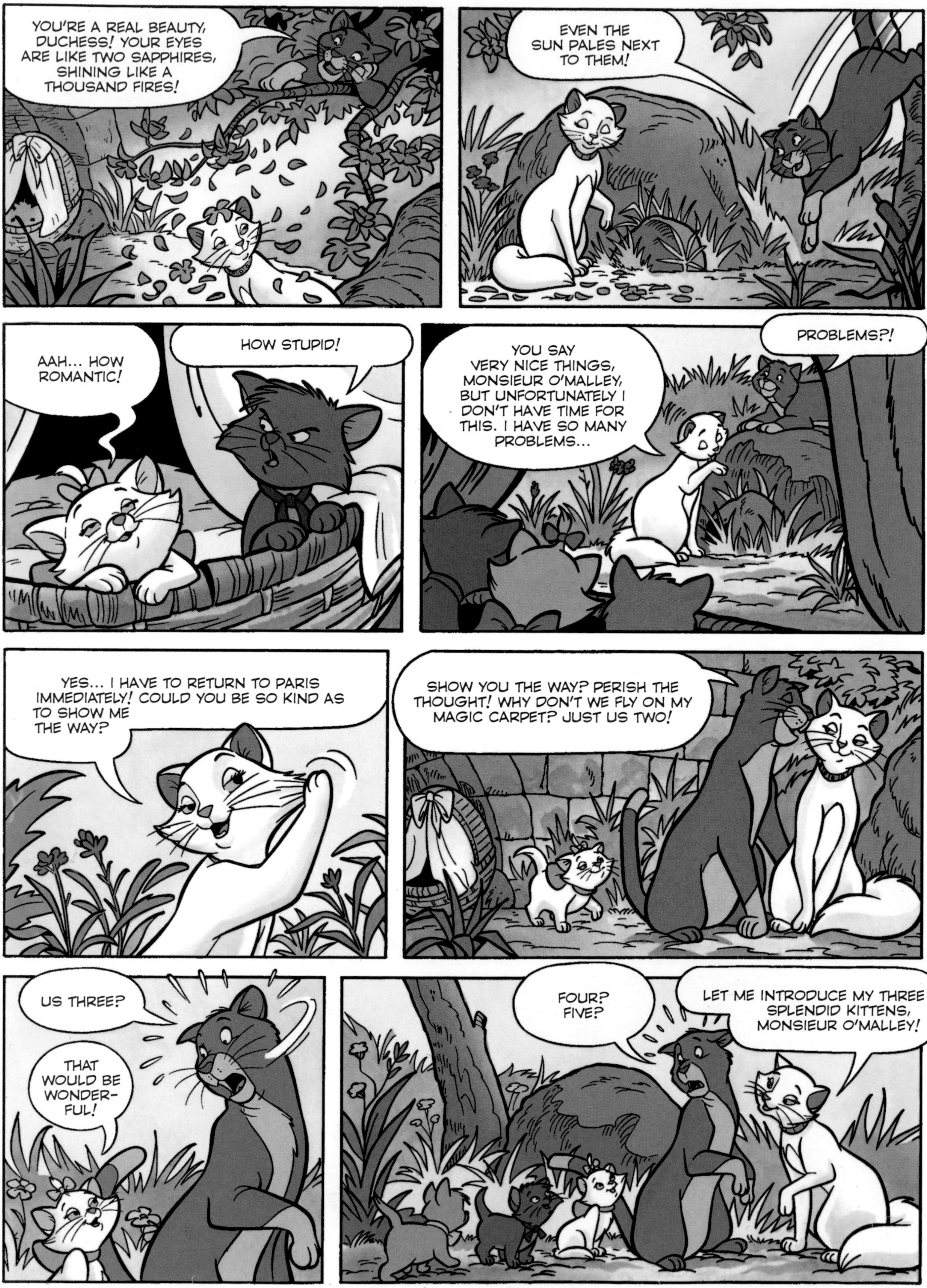
YOU'RE A REAL BEAUTY, DUCHESS! YOUR EYES ARE LIKE TWO SAPPHIRES, SHINING LIKE A THOUSAND FIRES!
EVEN THE SUN PALES NEXT TO THEM!
AAH... HOW ROMANTIC!
HOW STUPID!
YOU SAY VERY NICE THINGS, MONSIEUR O'MALLEY, BUT UNFORTUNATELY I DON'T HAVE TIME FOR THIS. I HAVE SO MANY PROBLEMS...
PROBLEMS?!
YES... I HAVE TO RETURN TO PARIS IMMEDIATELY! COULD YOU BE SO KIND AS TO SHOW ME THE WAY?
SHOW YOU THE WAY? PERISH THE THOUGHT! WHY DON'T WE FLY ON MY MAGIC CARPET? JUST US TWO!
US THREE?
THAT WOULD BE WONDER-FUL!
FOUR? FIVE?
LET ME INTRODUCE MY THREE SPLENDID KITTENS, MONSIEUR O'MALLEY!

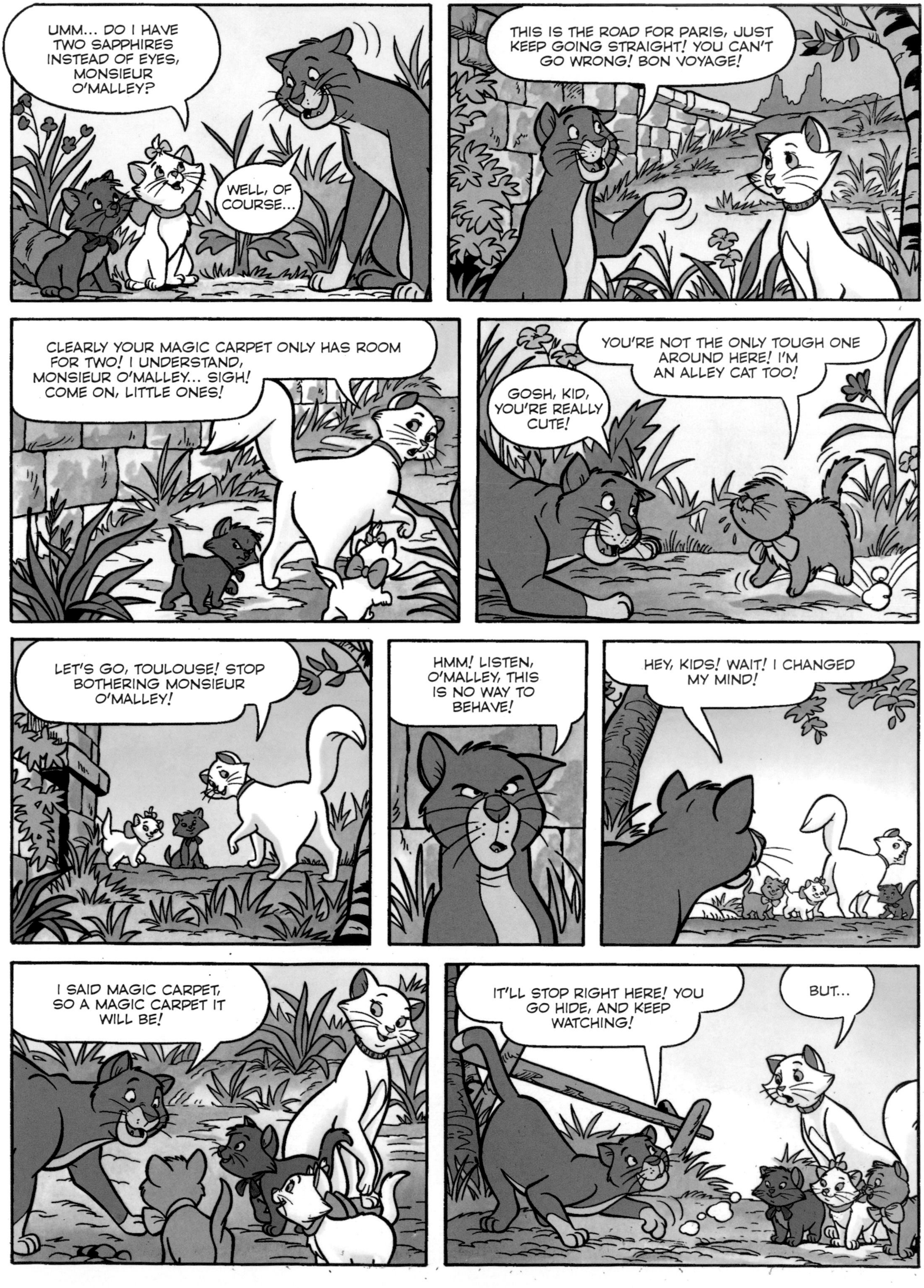
UMM... DO I HAVE TWO SAPPHIRES INSTEAD OF EYES, MONSIEUR O'MALLEY?
WELL, OF COURSE...
THIS IS THE ROAD FOR PARIS, JUST KEEP GOING STRAIGHT! YOU CAN'T GO WRONG! BON VOYAGE!
CLEARLY YOUR MAGIC CARPET ONLY HAS ROOM FOR TWO! I UNDERSTAND, MONSIEUR O'MALLEY... SIGH! COME ON, LITTLE ONES!
YOU'RE NOT THE ONLY TOUGH ONE AROUND HERE! I'M AN ALLEY CAT TOO!
GOSH, KID, YOU'RE REALLY CUTE!
LET'S GO, TOULOUSE! STOP BOTHERING MONSIEUR O'MALLEY!
HMM! LISTEN, O'MALLEY, THIS IS NO WAY TO BEHAVE!
HEY, KIDS! WAIT! I CHANGED MY MIND!
I SAID MAGIC CARPET, SO A MAGIC CARPET IT WILL BE!
IT'LL STOP RIGHT HERE! YOU GO HIDE, AND KEEP WATCHING!
BUT...

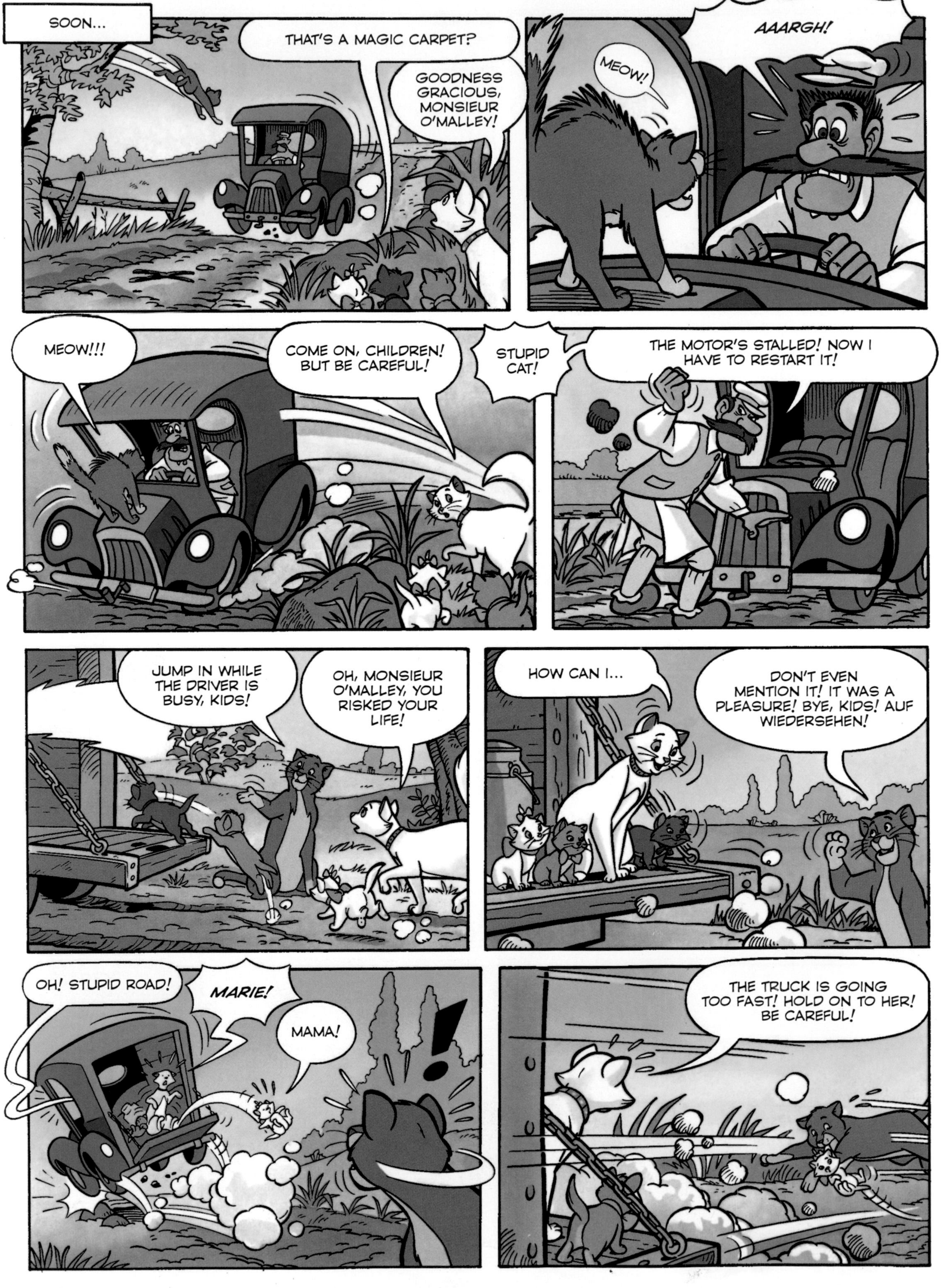

SOON...
THAT'S A MAGIC CARPET?
GOODNESS GRACIOUS, MONSIEUR O'MALLEY!
AAARGH!
MEOW!
MEOW!!!
COME ON, CHILDREN! BUT BE CAREFUL!
STUPID CAT!
THE MOTOR'S STALLED! NOW I HAVE TO RESTART IT!
JUMP IN WHILE THE DRIVER IS BUSY, KIDS!
OH, MONSIEUR O'MALLEY, YOU RISKED YOUR LIFE!
HOW CAN I...
DON'T EVEN MENTION IT! IT WAS A PLEASURE! BYE, KIDS! AUF WIEDERSEHEN!
OH! STUPID ROAD!
MARIE!
MAMA!
THE TRUCK IS GOING TOO FAST! HOLD ON TO HER! BE CAREFUL!

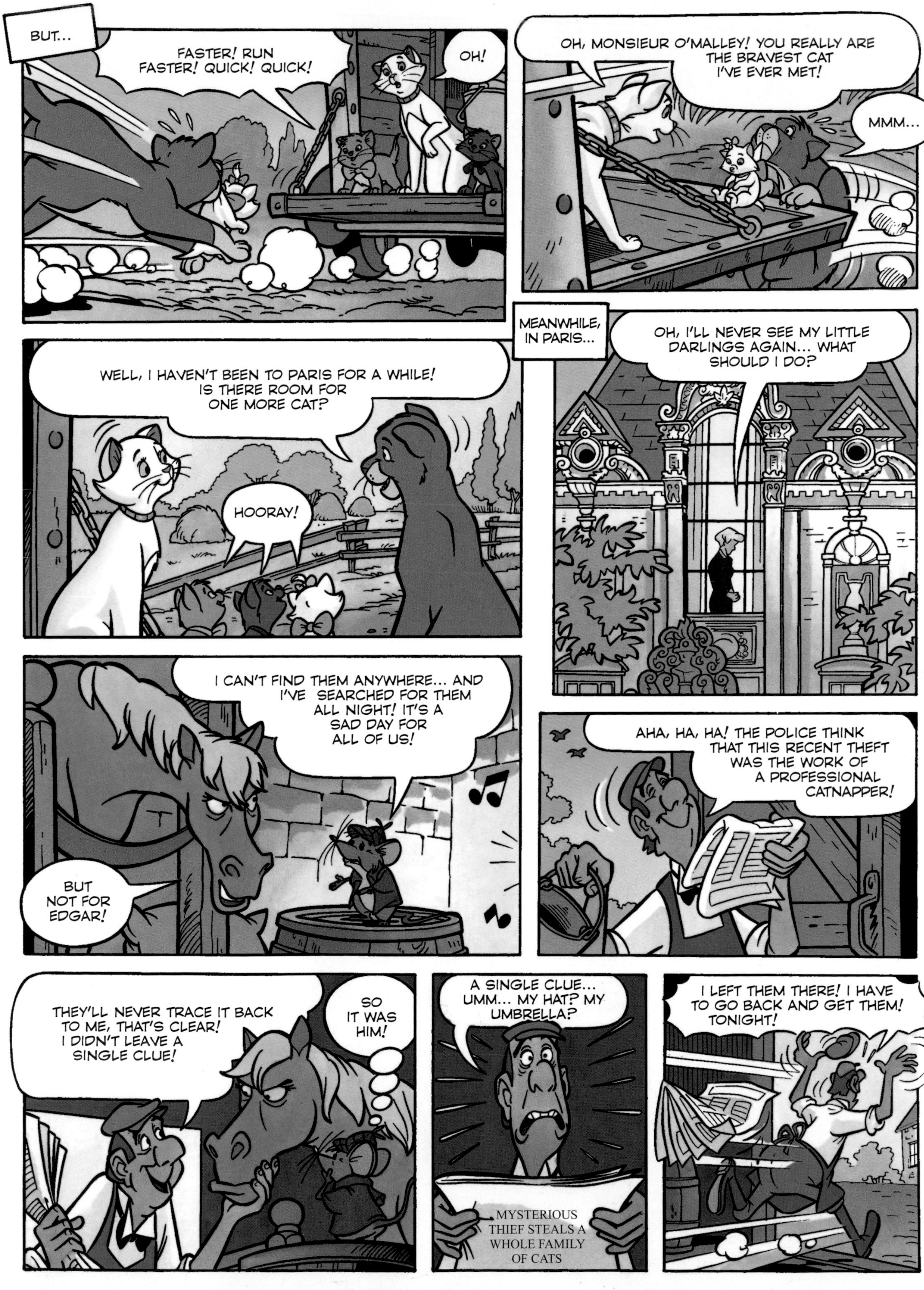
BUT...
FASTER! RUN FASTER! QUICK! QUICK!
OH!
OH, MONSIEUR O'MALLEY! YOU REALLY ARE THE BRAVEST CAT I'VE EVER MET!
MMM...
WELL, I HAVEN'T BEEN TO PARIS FOR A WHILE! IS THERE ROOM FOR ONE MORE CAT?
HOORAY!
MEANWHILE, IN PARIS...
OH, I'LL NEVER SEE MY LITTLE DARLINGS AGAIN... WHAT SHOULD I DO?
I CAN'T FIND THEM ANYWHERE... AND I'VE SEARCHED FOR THEM ALL NIGHT! IT'S A SAD DAY FOR ALL OF US!
BUT NOT FOR EDGAR!
AHA, HA, HA! THE POLICE THINK THAT THIS RECENT THEFT WAS THE WORK OF A PROFESSIONAL CATNAPPER!
THEY'LL NEVER TRACE IT BACK TO ME, THAT'S CLEAR! I DIDN'T LEAVE A SINGLE CLUE!
SO IT WAS HIM!
A SINGLE CLUE... UMM... MY HAT? MY UMBRELLA?
MYSTERIOUS THIEF STEALS A WHOLE FAMILY OF CATS
I LEFT THEM THERE! I HAVE TO GO BACK AND GET THEM! TONIGHT!

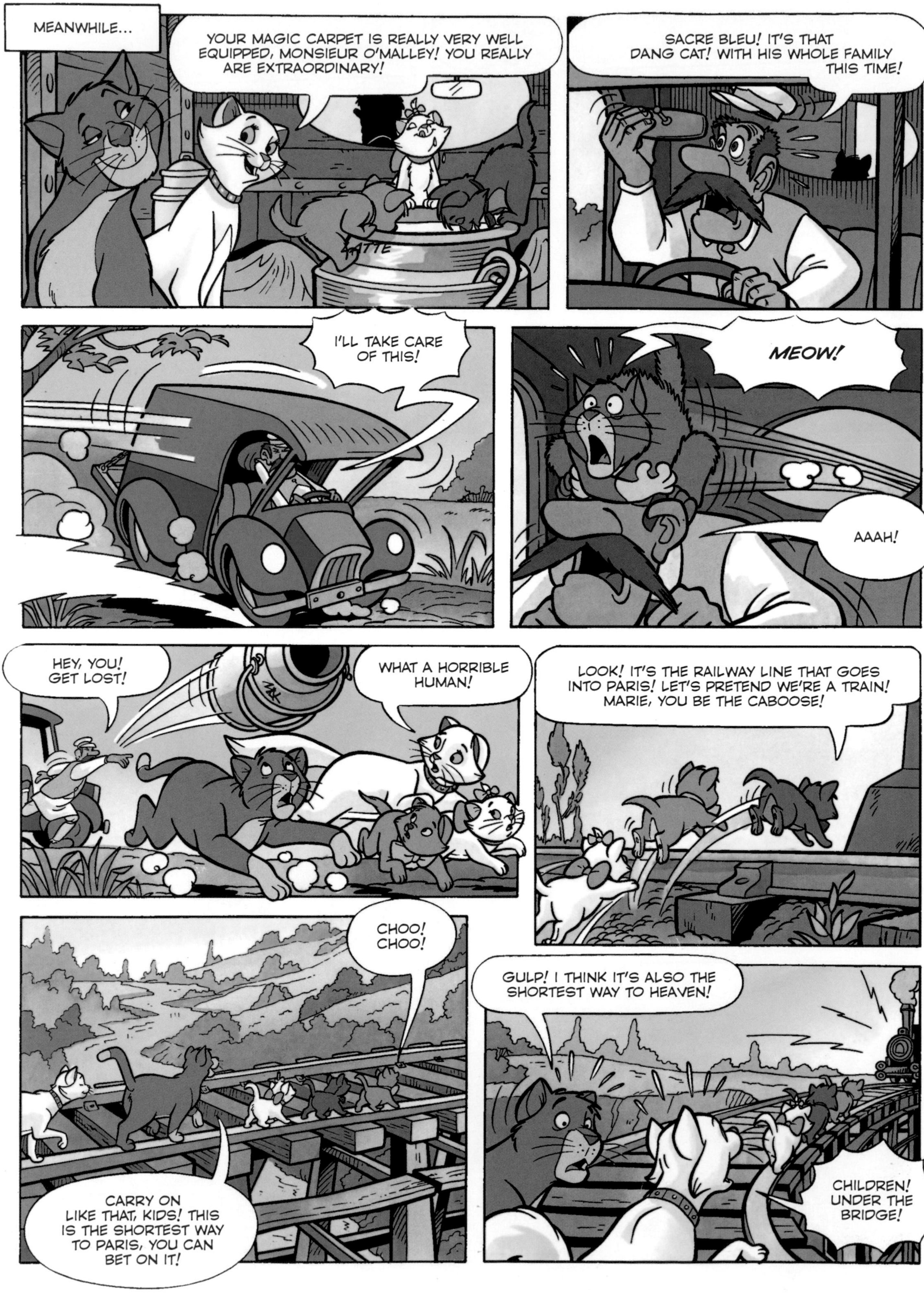
MEANWHILE...
YOUR MAGIC CARPET IS REALLY VERY WELL EQUIPPED, MONSIEUR O'MALLEY! YOU REALLY ARE EXTRAORDINARY!
SACRE BLEU! IT'S THAT DANG CAT! WITH HIS WHOLE FAMILY THIS TIME!
I'LL TAKE CARE OF THIS!
MEOW!
AAAH!
HEY, YOU! GET LOST!
WHAT A HORRIBLE HUMAN!
LOOK! IT'S THE RAILWAY LINE THAT GOES INTO PARIS! LET'S PRETEND WE'RE A TRAIN! MARIE, YOU BE THE CABOOSE!
CHOO! CHOO!
CARRY ON LIKE THAT, KIDS! THIS IS THE SHORTEST WAY TO PARIS, YOU CAN BET ON IT!
GULP! I THINK IT'S ALSO THE SHORTEST WAY TO HEAVEN!
CHILDREN! UNDER THE BRIDGE!

PHEW! THAT SMOKY OLD WRECK HAS PASSED! WE CAN GET BACK ON THE BRIDGE!

BUT...

MAMA!

MARIE!

OH, NO! THIS REALLY ISN'T HER LUCKY DAY!

HOLD ON, KIDS! I'LL BE BACK IN HALF A SECOND!

COME ON! THIS LOG WILL BE USEFUL!

THE CURRENT IS CARRYING US AWAY, MONSIEUR O'MALLEY!

I'M HERE, THOMAS! I'LL TAKE THE LITTLE ONE!

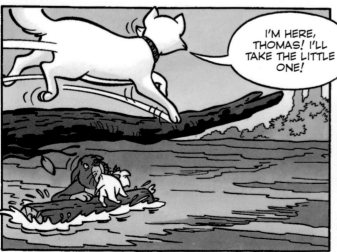

GOT HER!

OKAY... OOF... SEE YOU DOWN WHERE THE RIVER ENDS!

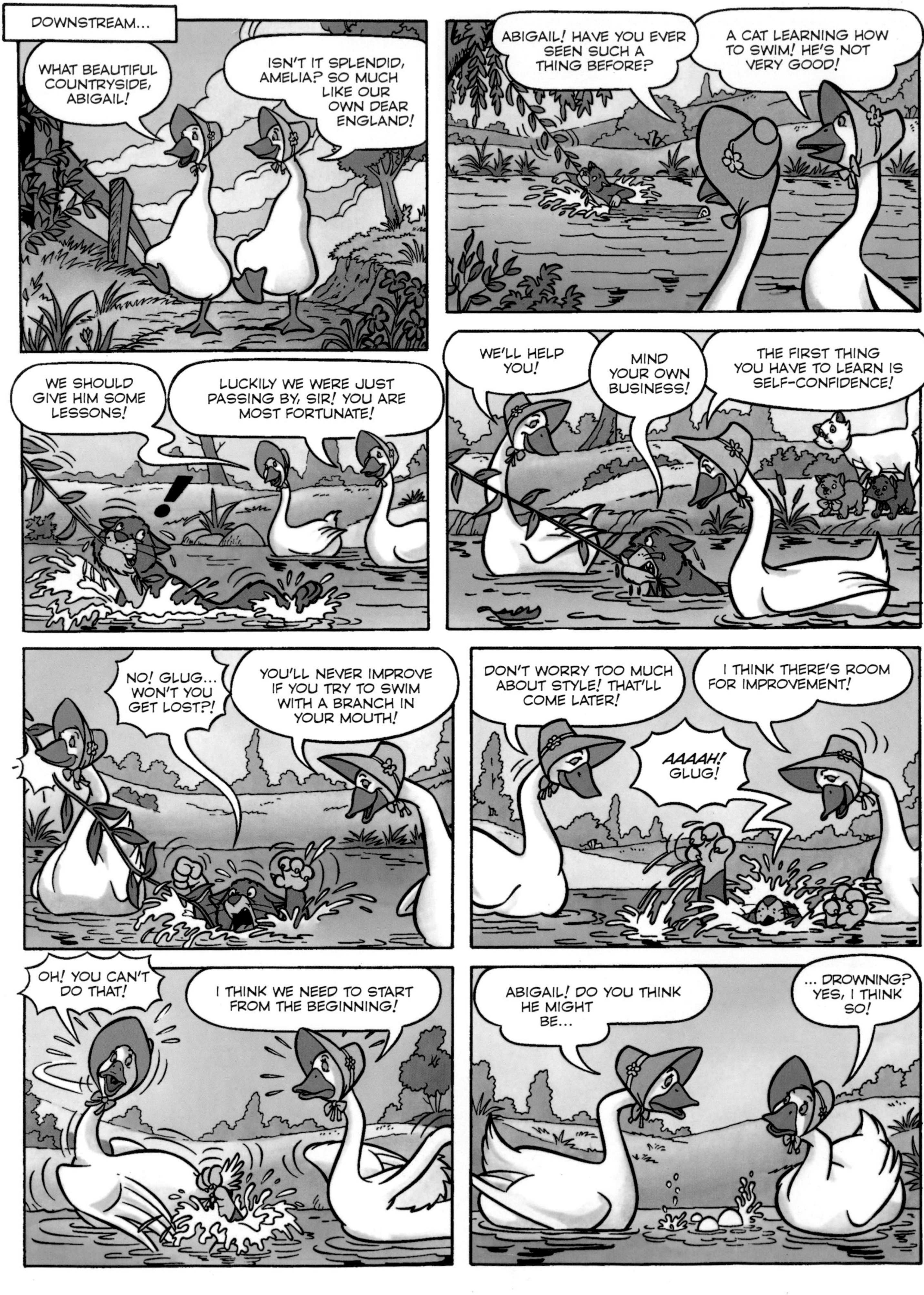
DOWNSTREAM...
WHAT BEAUTIFUL COUNTRYSIDE, ABIGAIL!
ISN'T IT SPLENDID, AMELIA? SO MUCH LIKE OUR OWN DEAR ENGLAND!
ABIGAIL! HAVE YOU EVER SEEN SUCH A THING BEFORE?
A CAT LEARNING HOW TO SWIM! HE'S NOT VERY GOOD!
WE SHOULD GIVE HIM SOME LESSONS!
LUCKILY WE WERE JUST PASSING BY, SIR! YOU ARE MOST FORTUNATE!
!
WE'LL HELP YOU!
MIND YOUR OWN BUSINESS!
THE FIRST THING YOU HAVE TO LEARN IS SELF-CONFIDENCE!
NO! GLUG... WON'T YOU GET LOST?!
YOU'LL NEVER IMPROVE IF YOU TRY TO SWIM WITH A BRANCH IN YOUR MOUTH!
DON'T WORRY TOO MUCH ABOUT STYLE! THAT'LL COME LATER!
AAAAH! GLUG!
I THINK THERE'S ROOM FOR IMPROVEMENT!
OH! YOU CAN'T DO THAT!
I THINK WE NEED TO START FROM THE BEGINNING!
ABIGAIL! DO YOU THINK HE MIGHT BE...
... DROWNING? YES, I THINK SO!

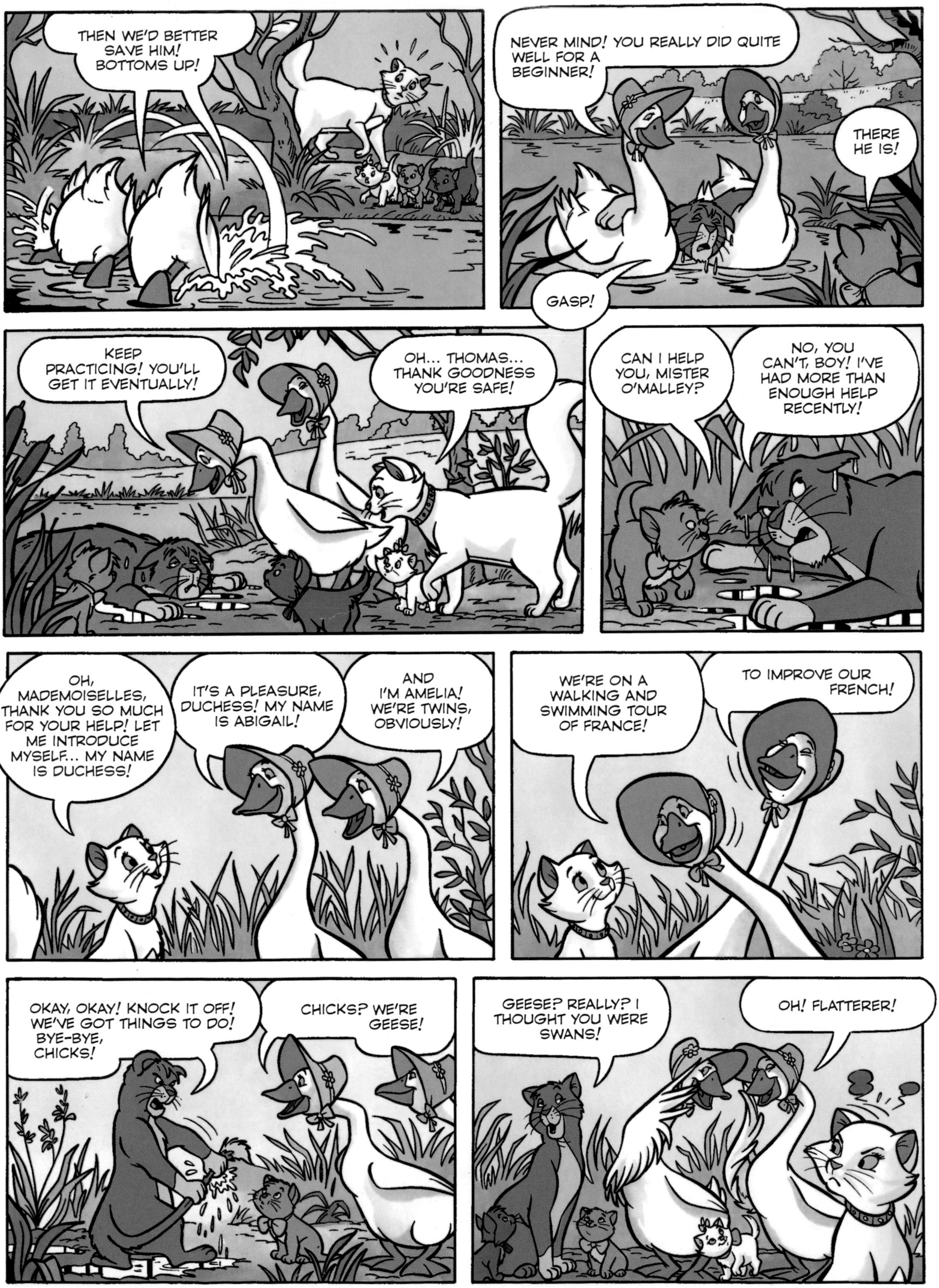

THEN WE'D BETTER SAVE HIM! BOTTOMS UP!
NEVER MIND! YOU REALLY DID QUITE WELL FOR A BEGINNER!
THERE HE IS!
GASP!
KEEP PRACTICING! YOU'LL GET IT EVENTUALLY!
OH... THOMAS... THANK GOODNESS YOU'RE SAFE!
CAN I HELP YOU, MISTER O'MALLEY?
NO, YOU CAN'T, BOY! I'VE HAD MORE THAN ENOUGH HELP RECENTLY!
OH, MADEMOISELLES, THANK YOU SO MUCH FOR YOUR HELP! LET ME INTRODUCE MYSELF... MY NAME IS DUCHESS!
IT'S A PLEASURE, DUCHESS! MY NAME IS ABIGAIL!
AND I'M AMELIA! WE'RE TWINS, OBVIOUSLY!
WE'RE ON A WALKING AND SWIMMING TOUR OF FRANCE!
TO IMPROVE OUR FRENCH!
OKAY, OKAY! KNOCK IT OFF! WE'VE GOT THINGS TO DO! BYE-BYE, CHICKS!
CHICKS? WE'RE GEESE!
GEESE? REALLY? I THOUGHT YOU WERE SWANS!
OH! FLATTERER!

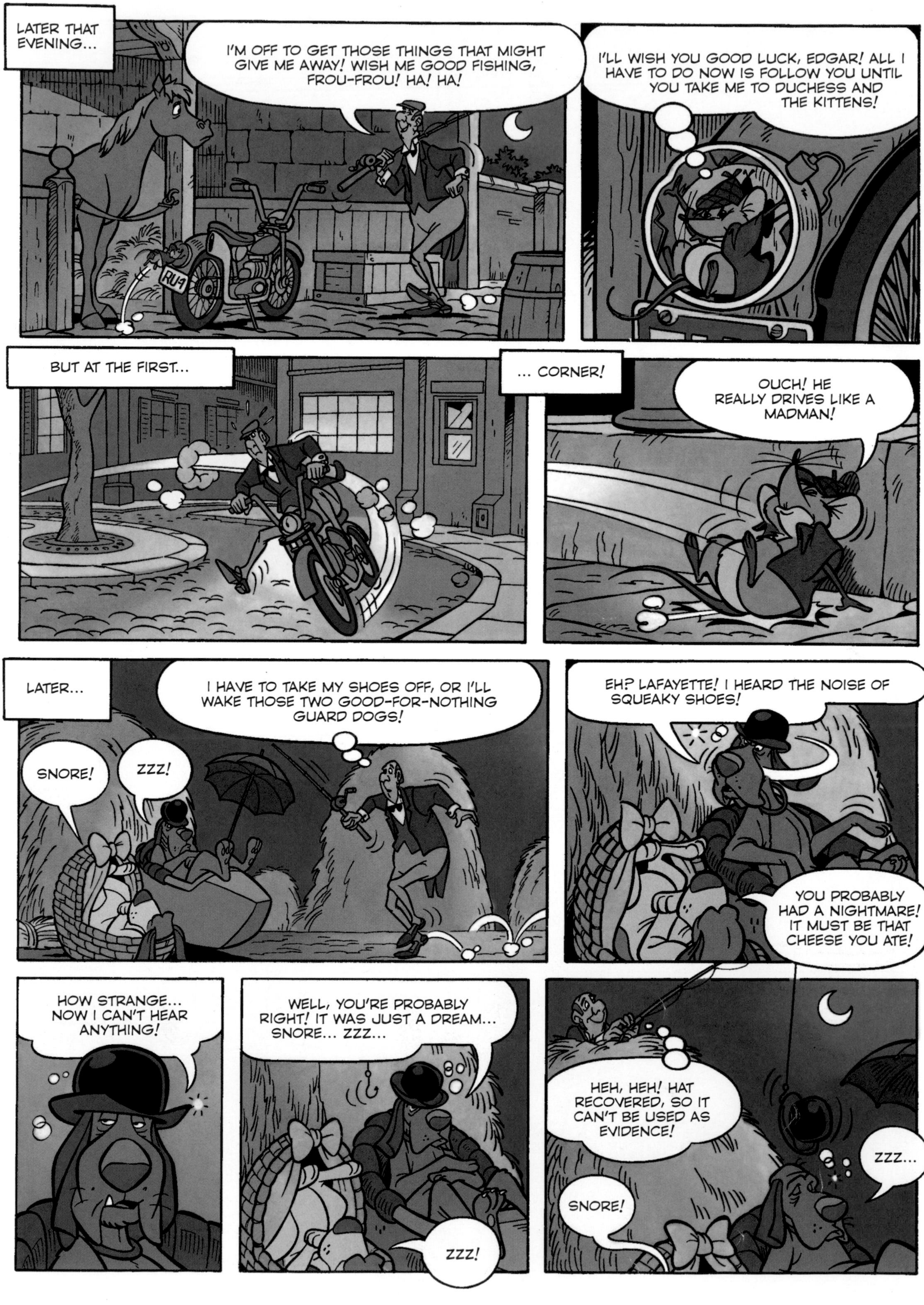
LATER THAT EVENING...
I'M OFF TO GET THOSE THINGS THAT MIGHT GIVE ME AWAY! WISH ME GOOD FISHING, FROU-FROU! HA! HA!
RU9
I'LL WISH YOU GOOD LUCK, EDGAR! ALL I HAVE TO DO NOW IS FOLLOW YOU UNTIL YOU TAKE ME TO DUCHESS AND THE KITTENS!
BUT AT THE FIRST...
... CORNER!
OUCH! HE REALLY DRIVES LIKE A MADMAN!
LATER...
I HAVE TO TAKE MY SHOES OFF, OR I'LL WAKE THOSE TWO GOOD-FOR-NOTHING GUARD DOGS!
SNORE!
ZZZ!
EH? LAFAYETTE! I HEARD THE NOISE OF SQUEAKY SHOES!
YOU PROBABLY HAD A NIGHTMARE! IT MUST BE THAT CHEESE YOU ATE!
HOW STRANGE... NOW I CAN'T HEAR ANYTHING!
WELL, YOU'RE PROBABLY RIGHT! IT WAS JUST A DREAM... SNORE... ZZZ...
ZZZ!
HEH, HEH! HAT RECOVERED, SO IT CAN'T BE USED AS EVIDENCE!
ZZZ...
SNORE!

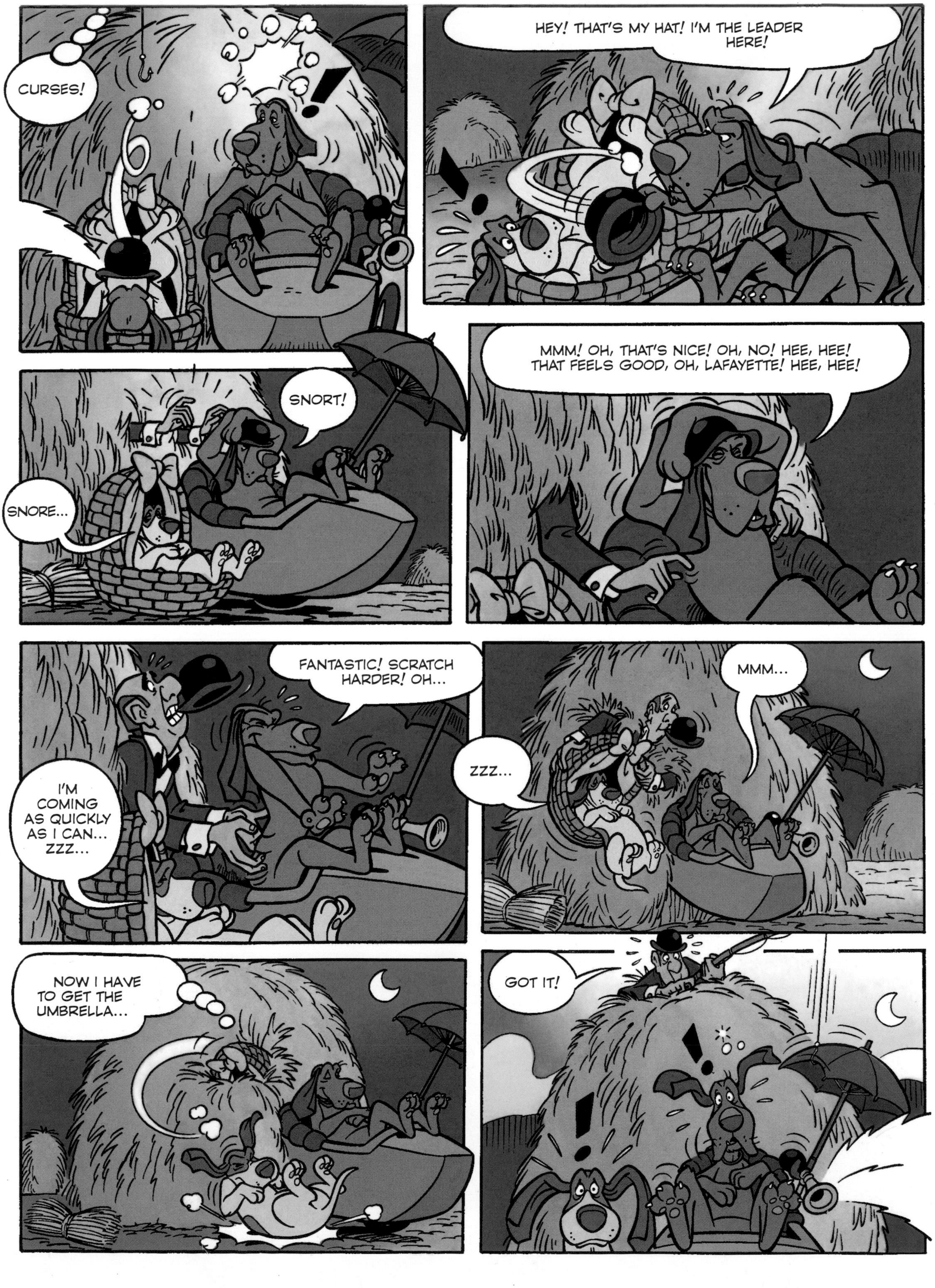
CURSES!
HEY! THAT'S MY HAT! I'M THE LEADER HERE!
SNORT!
SNORE...
MMM! OH, THAT'S NICE! OH, NO! HEE, HEE! THAT FEELS GOOD, OH, LAFAYETTE! HEE, HEE!
FANTASTIC! SCRATCH HARDER! OH...
I'M COMING AS QUICKLY AS I CAN... ZZZ...
MMM...
ZZZ...
NOW I HAVE TO GET THE UMBRELLA...
GOT IT!

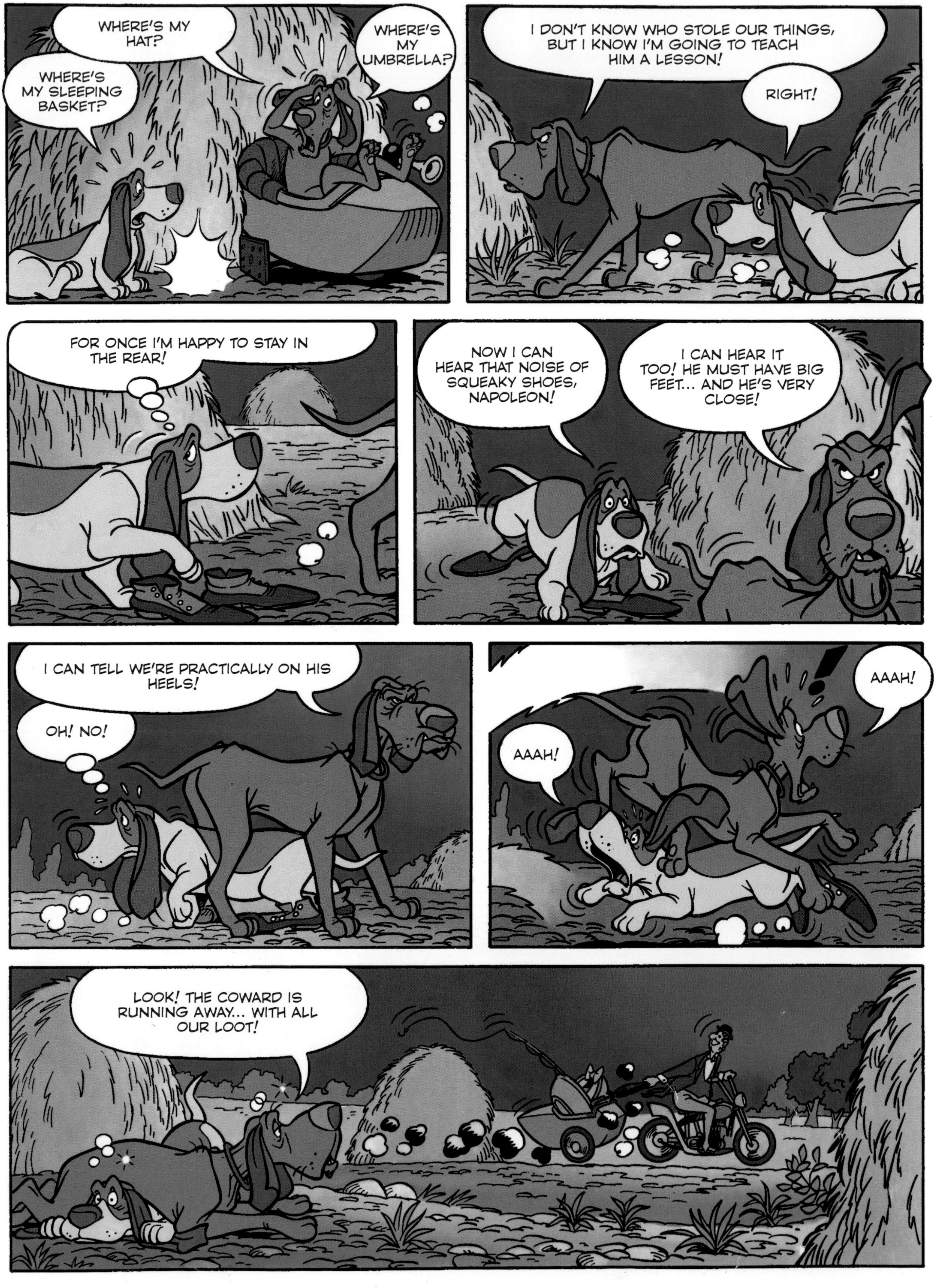
WHERE'S MY HAT?
WHERE'S MY SLEEPING BASKET?
WHERE'S MY UMBRELLA?
I DON'T KNOW WHO STOLE OUR THINGS, BUT I KNOW I'M GOING TO TEACH HIM A LESSON!
RIGHT!
FOR ONCE I'M HAPPY TO STAY IN THE REAR!
NOW I CAN HEAR THAT NOISE OF SQUEAKY SHOES, NAPOLEON!
I CAN HEAR IT TOO! HE MUST HAVE BIG FEET... AND HE'S VERY CLOSE!
I CAN TELL WE'RE PRACTICALLY ON HIS HEELS!
OH! NO!
AAAH!
AAAH!
LOOK! THE COWARD IS RUNNING AWAY... WITH ALL OUR LOOT!

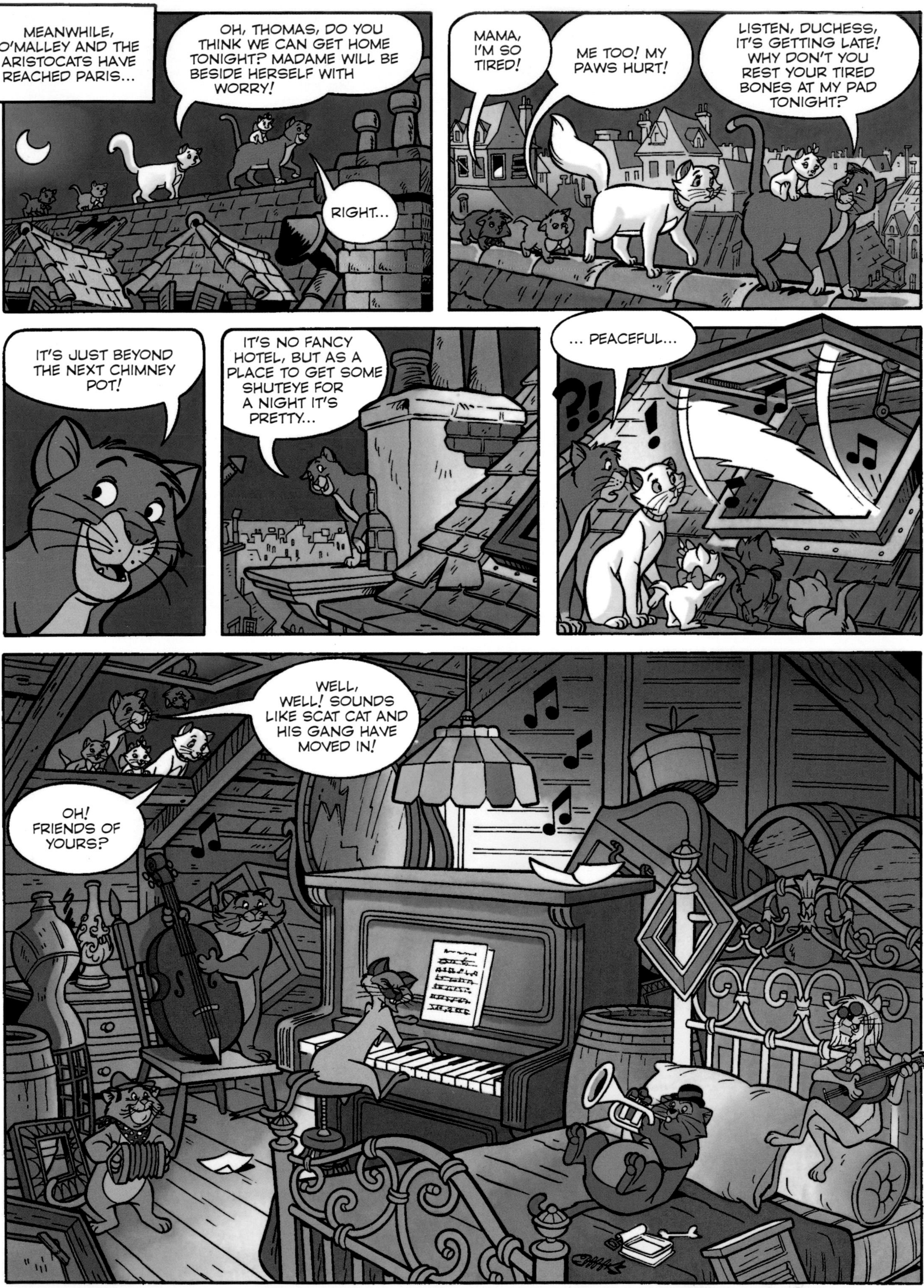
MEANWHILE, O'MALLEY AND THE ARISTOCATS HAVE REACHED PARIS...
OH, THOMAS, DO YOU THINK WE CAN GET HOME TONIGHT? MADAME WILL BE BESIDE HERSELF WITH WORRY!
RIGHT...
MAMA, I'M SO TIRED!
ME TOO! MY PAWS HURT!
LISTEN, DUCHESS, IT'S GETTING LATE! WHY DON'T YOU REST YOUR TIRED BONES AT MY PAD TONIGHT?
IT'S JUST BEYOND THE NEXT CHIMNEY POT!
IT'S NO FANCY HOTEL, BUT AS A PLACE TO GET SOME SHUTEYE FOR A NIGHT IT'S PRETTY...
... PEACEFUL...
?!
!
WELL, WELL! SOUNDS LIKE SCAT CAT AND HIS GANG HAVE MOVED IN!
OH! FRIENDS OF YOURS?

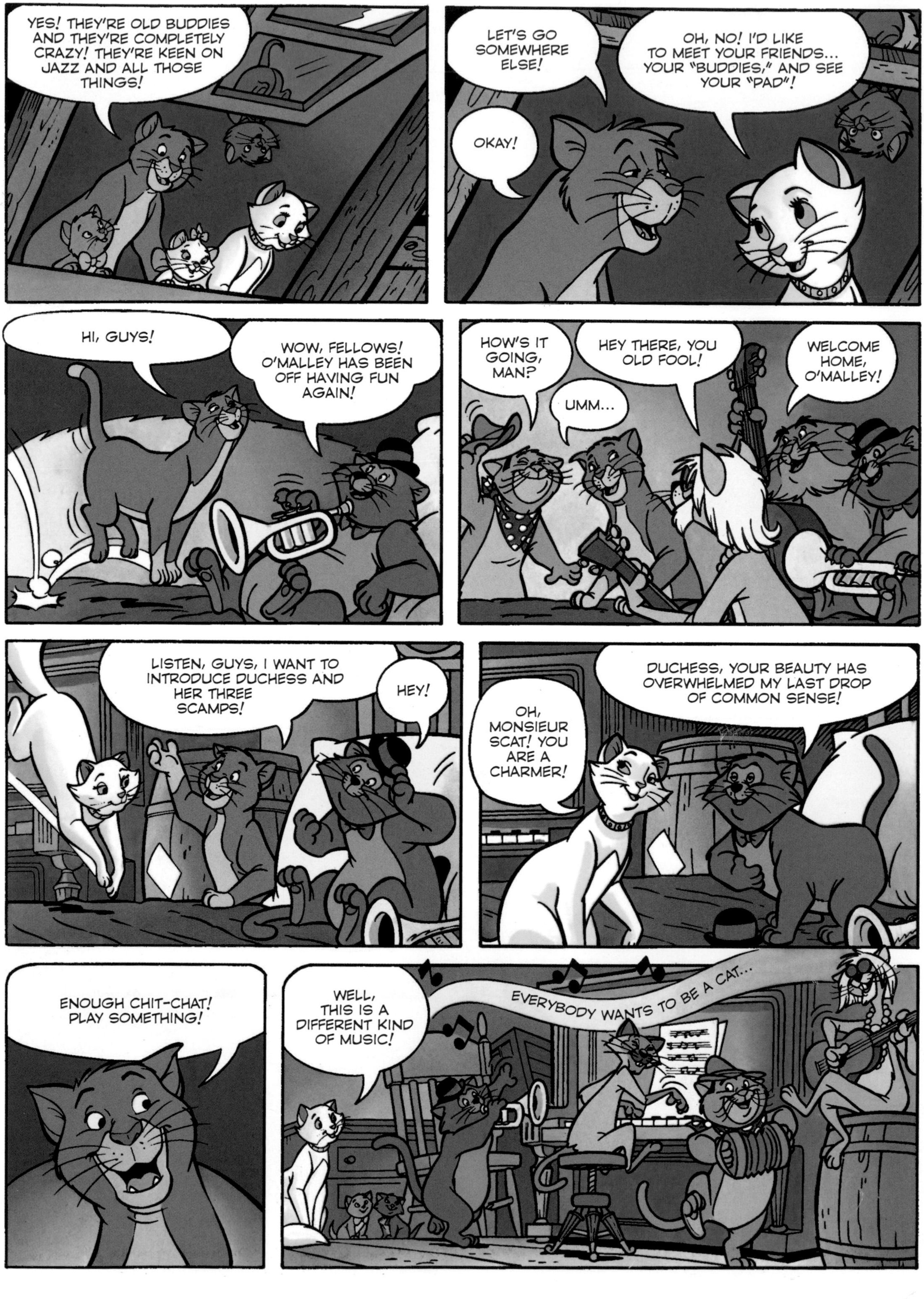
YES! THEY'RE OLD BUDDIES AND THEY'RE COMPLETELY CRAZY! THEY'RE KEEN ON JAZZ AND ALL THOSE THINGS!
LET'S GO SOMEWHERE ELSE!
OH, NO! I'D LIKE TO MEET YOUR FRIENDS... YOUR "BUDDIES," AND SEE YOUR "PAD"!
OKAY!
HI, GUYS!
WOW, FELLOWS! O'MALLEY HAS BEEN OFF HAVING FUN AGAIN!
HOW'S IT GOING, MAN?
HEY THERE, YOU OLD FOOL!
UMM...
WELCOME HOME, O'MALLEY!
LISTEN, GUYS, I WANT TO INTRODUCE DUCHESS AND HER THREE SCAMPS!
HEY!
DUCHESS, YOUR BEAUTY HAS OVERWHELMED MY LAST DROP OF COMMON SENSE!
OH, MONSIEUR SCAT! YOU ARE A CHARMER!
ENOUGH CHIT-CHAT! PLAY SOMETHING!
WELL, THIS IS A DIFFERENT KIND OF MUSIC!
EVERYBODY WANTS TO BE A CAT...

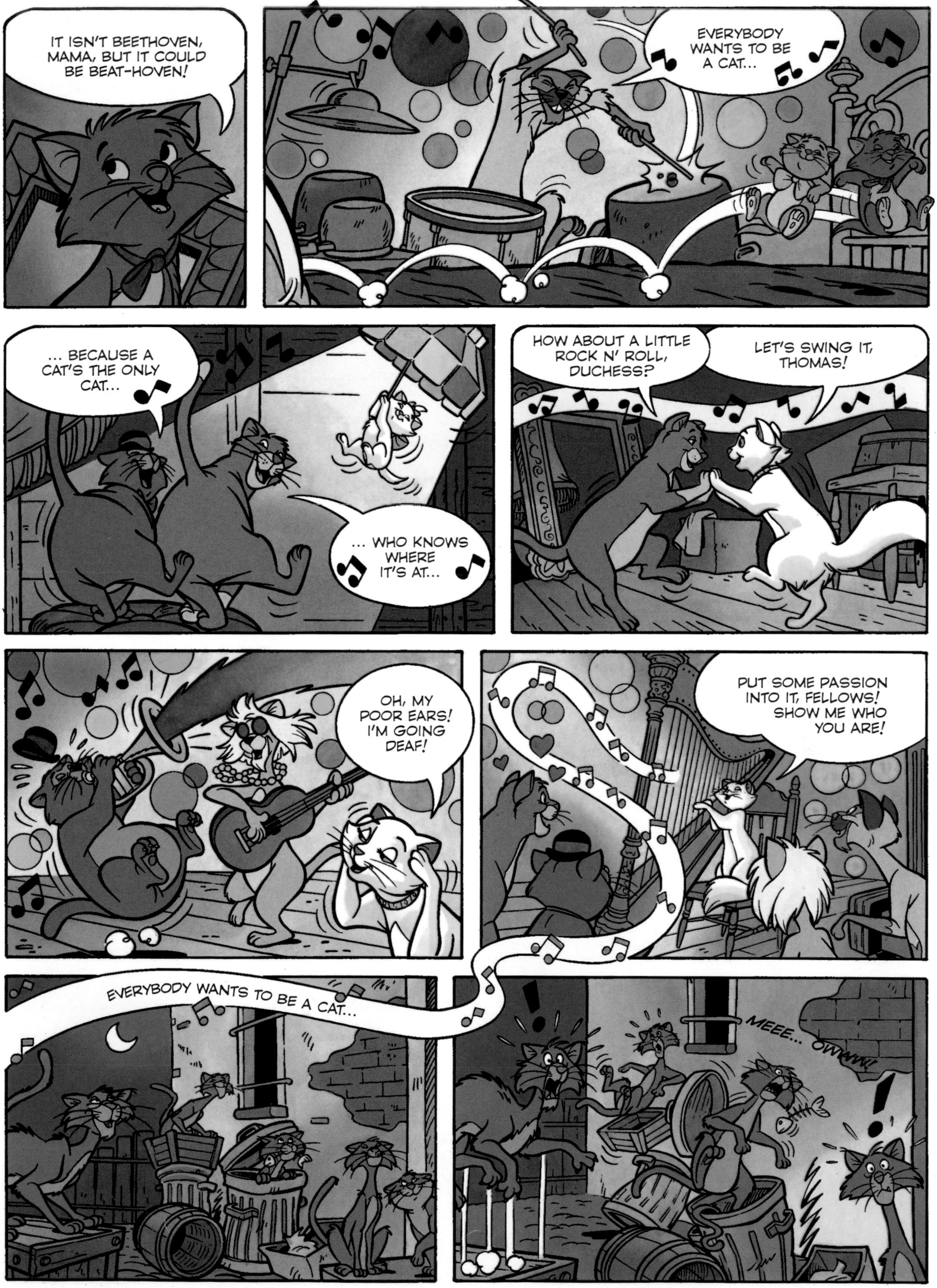
IT ISN'T BEETHOVEN, MAMA, BUT IT COULD BE BEAT-HOVEN!
EVERYBODY WANTS TO BE A CAT...
... BECAUSE A CAT'S THE ONLY CAT...
... WHO KNOWS WHERE IT'S AT...
HOW ABOUT A LITTLE ROCK N' ROLL, DUCHESS?
LET'S SWING IT, THOMAS!
OH, MY POOR EARS! I'M GOING DEAF!
PUT SOME PASSION INTO IT, FELLOWS! SHOW ME WHO YOU ARE!
EVERYBODY WANTS TO BE A CAT...
MEEE... OWWW!

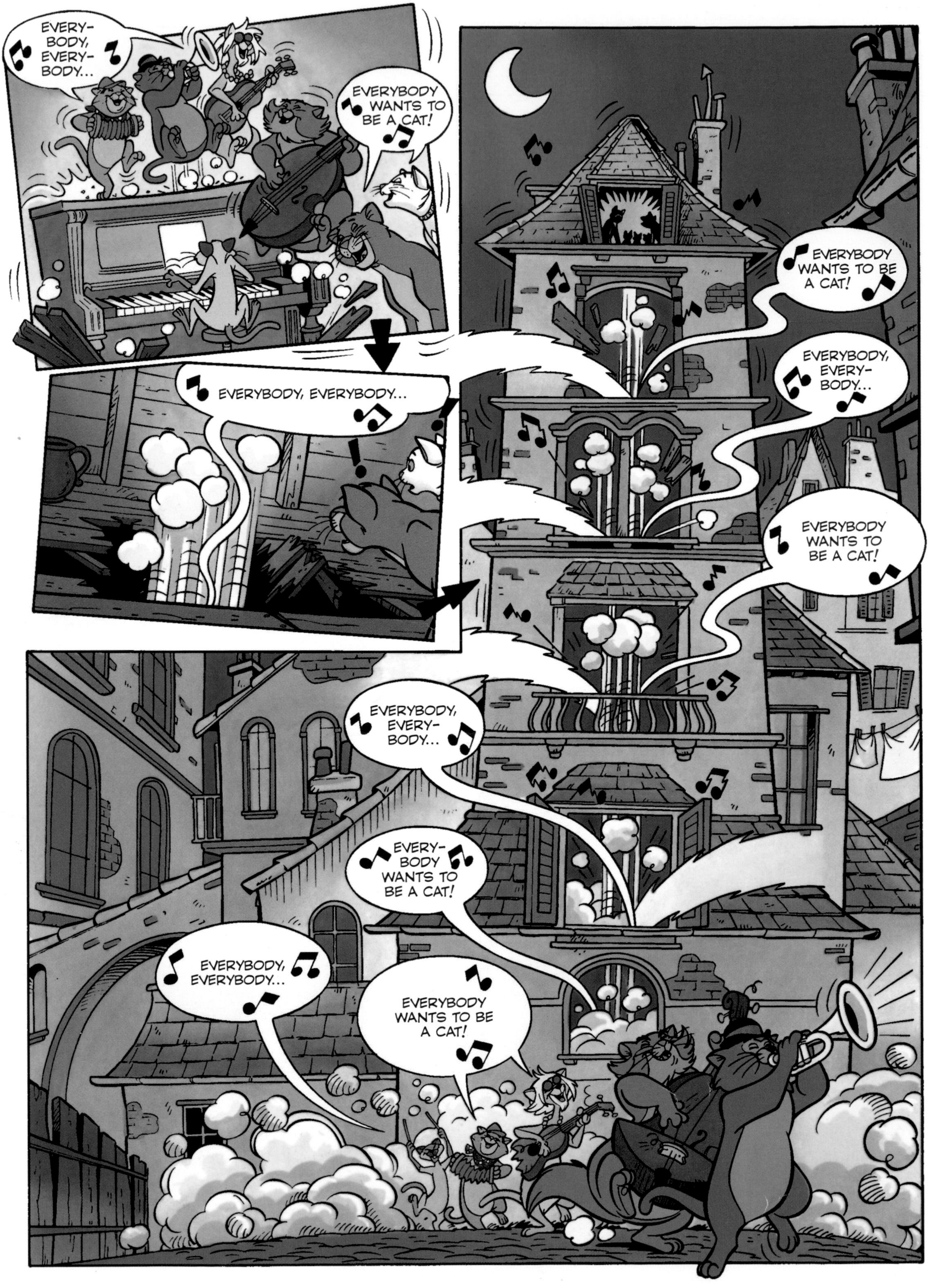
EVERY-BODY, EVERY-BODY...
EVERYBODY WANTS TO BE A CAT!
EVERYBODY, EVERYBODY...
EVERYBODY WANTS TO BE A CAT!
EVERYBODY, EVERY-BODY...
EVERYBODY WANTS TO BE A CAT!
EVERYBODY, EVERY-BODY...
EVERY-BODY WANTS TO BE A CAT!
EVERYBODY, EVERYBODY...
EVERYBODY WANTS TO BE A CAT!

AND WHEN IT'S ALL FINALLY OVER...

EVERYBODY... EVERYBODY...

ZZZ...

SWEET DREAMS, MY LOVES!

YOUR FRIENDS ARE REALLY DELIGHTFUL, THOMAS!

YES, THEY'RE REALLY A GREAT GROUP, DUCHY! WHEN YOU'RE IN TROUBLE, YOU KNOW YOU CAN COUNT ON THEM!

LIKE I CAN COUNT ON YOU, THOMAS!

COME! MAMA'S TALKING TO MISTER O'MALLEY!

THANK YOU SO MUCH FOR MAKING US FEEL WELCOME IN YOUR PAD!

IT'S NOTHING!

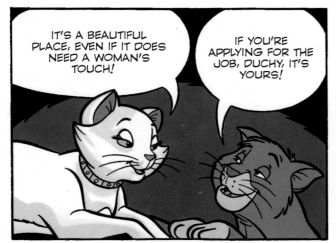

IT'S A BEAUTIFUL PLACE, EVEN IF IT DOES NEED A WOMAN'S TOUCH!

IF YOU'RE APPLYING FOR THE JOB, DUCHY, IT'S YOURS!

GOODY! MOTHER'S GOING TO WORK FOR MISTER O'MALLEY!

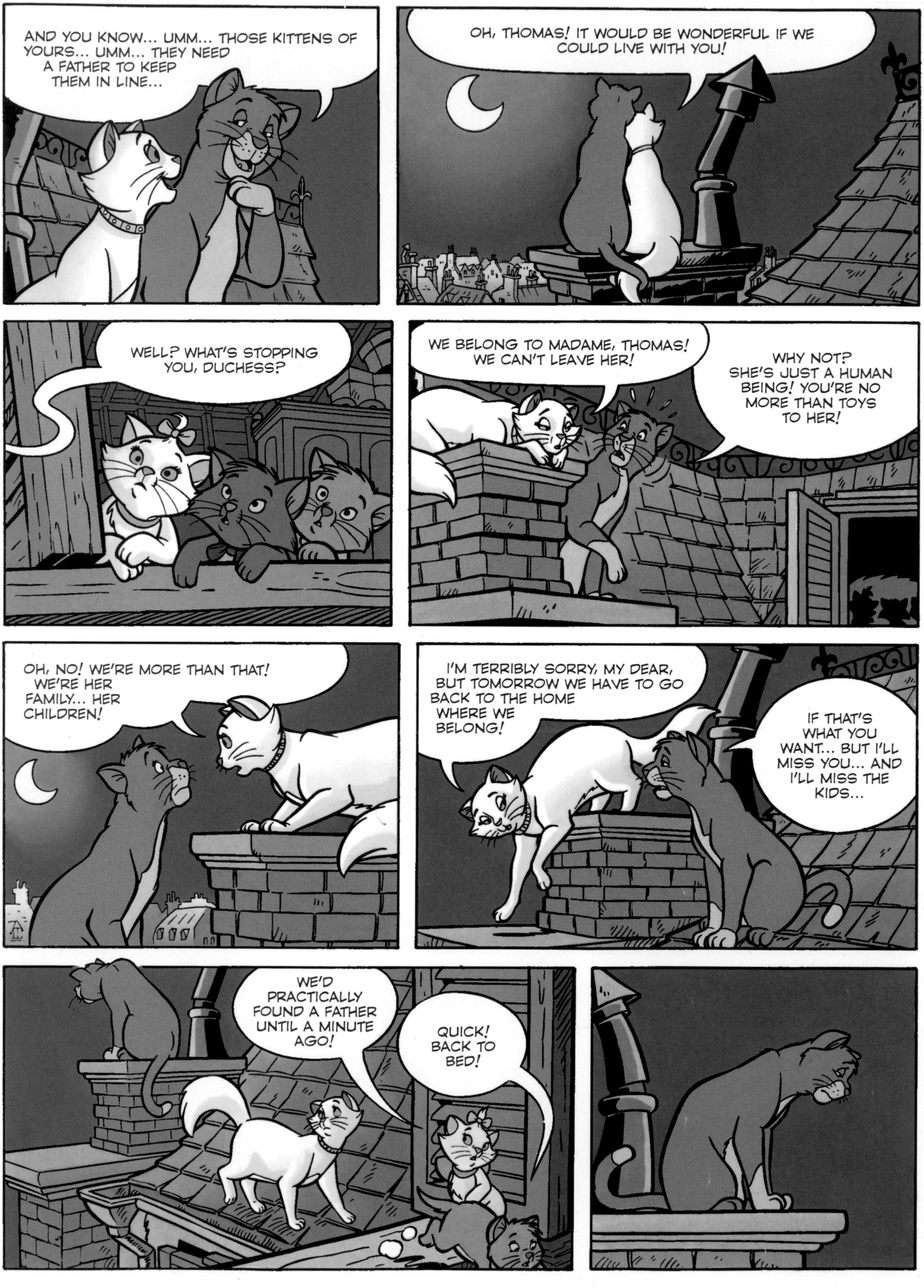
AND YOU KNOW... UMM... THOSE KITTENS OF YOURS... UMM... THEY NEED A FATHER TO KEEP THEM IN LINE...
OH, THOMAS! IT WOULD BE WONDERFUL IF WE COULD LIVE WITH YOU!
WELL? WHAT'S STOPPING YOU, DUCHESS?
WE BELONG TO MADAME, THOMAS! WE CAN'T LEAVE HER!
WHY NOT? SHE'S JUST A HUMAN BEING! YOU'RE NO MORE THAN TOYS TO HER!
OH, NO! WE'RE MORE THAN THAT! WE'RE HER FAMILY... HER CHILDREN!
I'M TERRIBLY SORRY, MY DEAR, BUT TOMORROW WE HAVE TO GO BACK TO THE HOME WHERE WE BELONG!
IF THAT'S WHAT YOU WANT... BUT I'LL MISS YOU... AND I'LL MISS THE KIDS...
WE'D PRACTICALLY FOUND A FATHER UNTIL A MINUTE AGO!
QUICK! BACK TO BED!

AND SO, THE NEXT MORNING AT DAWN...

CRIPES! ARE YOU SURE THIS IS REALLY YOUR NEIGHBORHOOD OR ARE YOU TAKING ME FOR A RIDE?

OF COURSE NOT! THAT HOUSE AT THE END OF THE STREET IS MADAME'S!

LOOK! WE'RE HOME!

HOORAY! YOU'RE FINALLY BACK!

EDGAR, OLD CHAP, YOU'LL SOON BE VERY RICH! ALL THAT MONEY, THOSE JEWELS! HA! HA! HA!

EDGAR! I FORGOT ABOUT HIM!

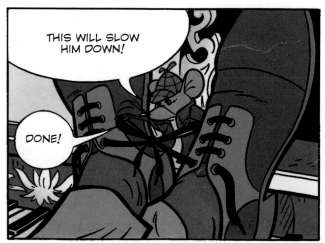

THIS WILL SLOW HIM DOWN!

DONE!

AAAH! HE SHOT ME!

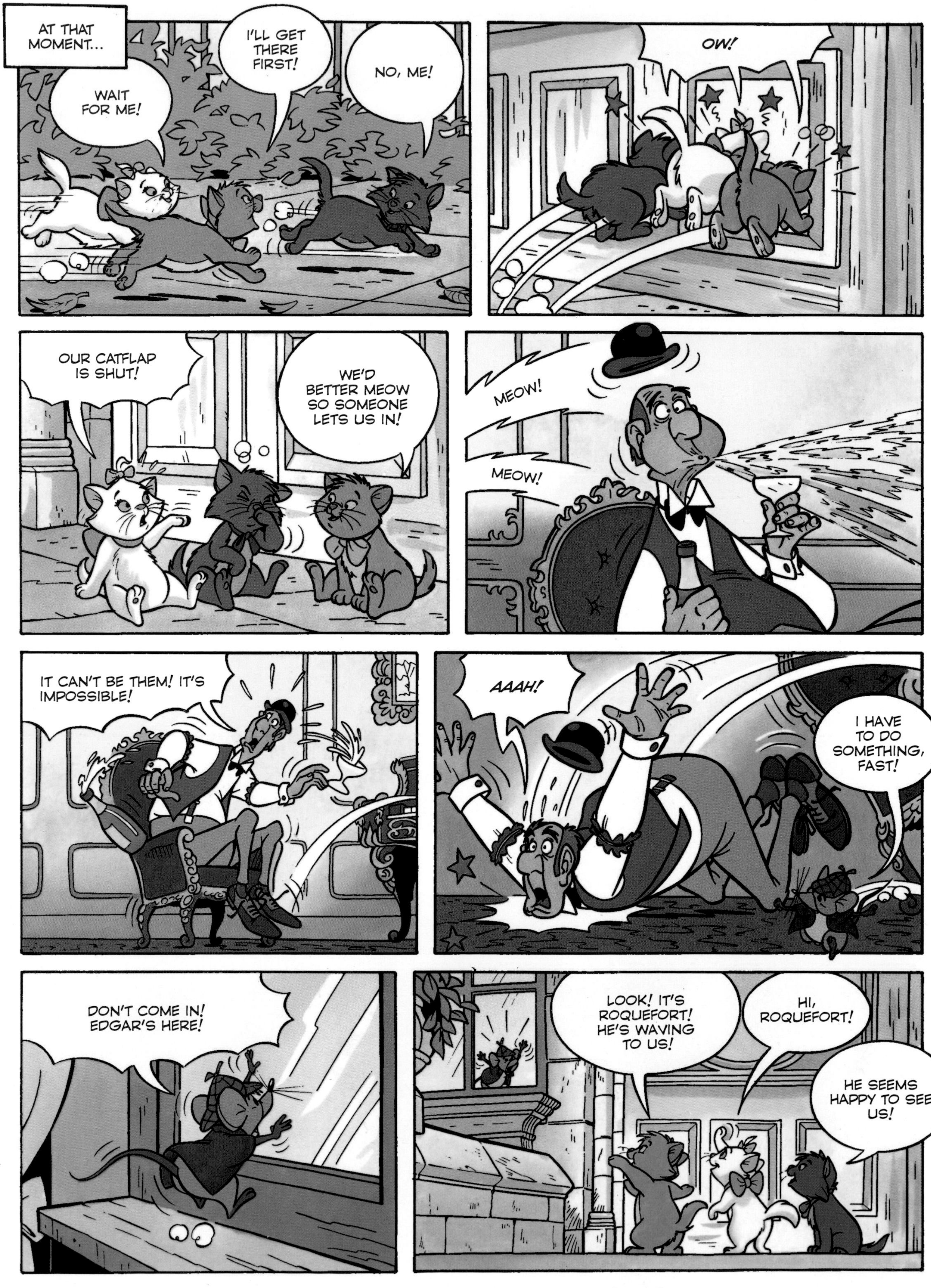
AT THAT MOMENT...
WAIT FOR ME!
I'LL GET THERE FIRST!
NO, ME!
OW!
OUR CATFLAP IS SHUT!
WE'D BETTER MEOW SO SOMEONE LETS US IN!
MEOW!
MEOW!
IT CAN'T BE THEM! IT'S IMPOSSIBLE!
AAAH!
I HAVE TO DO SOMETHING, FAST!
DON'T COME IN! EDGAR'S HERE!
LOOK! IT'S ROQUEFORT! HE'S WAVING TO US!
HI, ROQUEFORT!
HE SEEMS HAPPY TO SEE US!

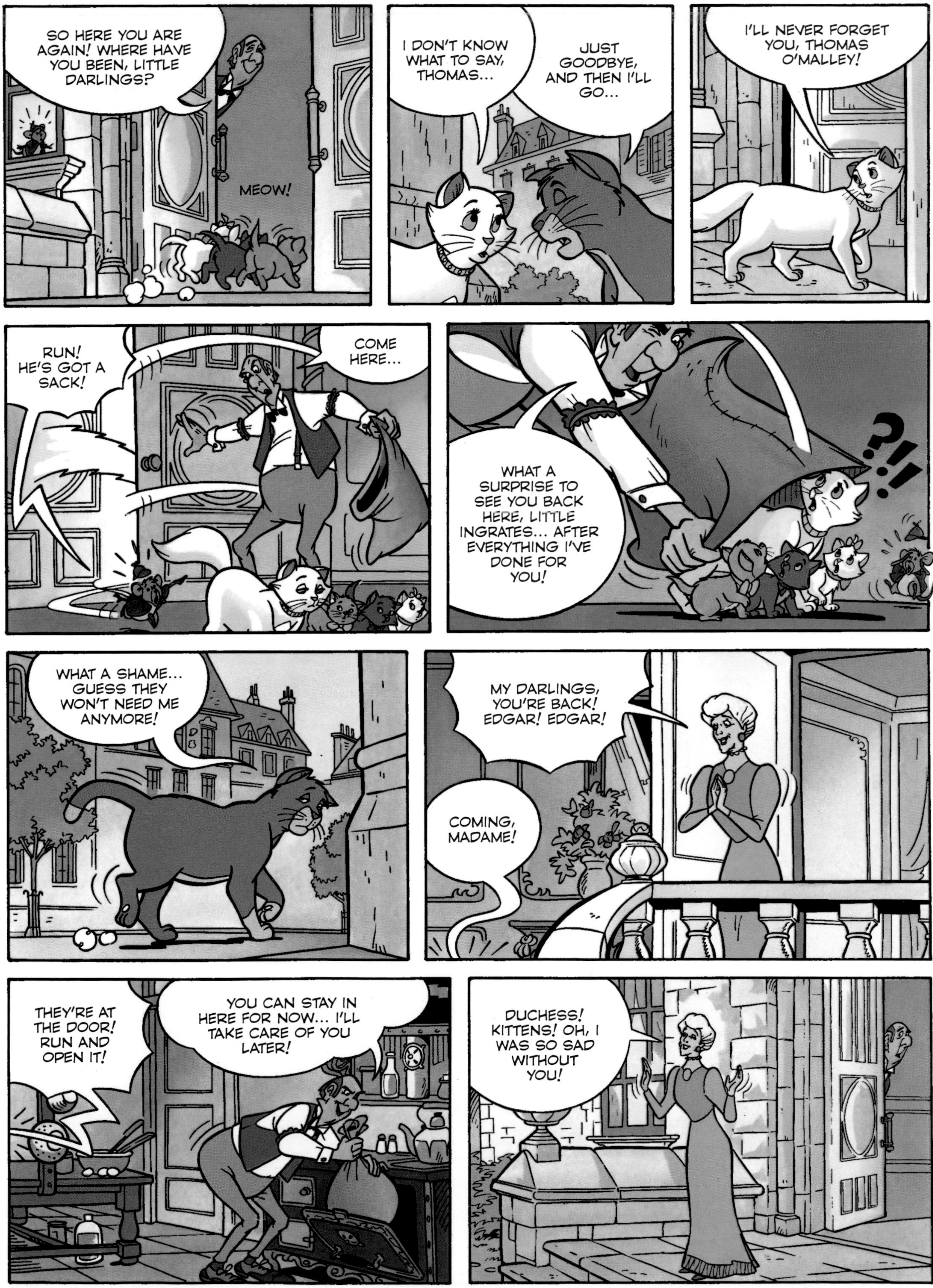
SO HERE YOU ARE AGAIN! WHERE HAVE YOU BEEN, LITTLE DARLINGS?
MEOW!
I DON'T KNOW WHAT TO SAY, THOMAS...
JUST GOODBYE, AND THEN I'LL GO...
I'LL NEVER FORGET YOU, THOMAS O'MALLEY!
RUN! HE'S GOT A SACK!
COME HERE...
WHAT A SURPRISE TO SEE YOU BACK HERE, LITTLE INGRATES... AFTER EVERYTHING I'VE DONE FOR YOU!
?!!
WHAT A SHAME... GUESS THEY WON'T NEED ME ANYMORE!
MY DARLINGS, YOU'RE BACK! EDGAR! EDGAR!
COMING, MADAME!
THEY'RE AT THE DOOR! RUN AND OPEN IT!
YOU CAN STAY IN HERE FOR NOW... I'LL TAKE CARE OF YOU LATER!
DUCHESS! KITTENS! OH, I WAS SO SAD WITHOUT YOU!

COME HERE, MY DARLINGS!

AHEM! SHOULD I CALL THEM, MADAME?

KITTENS! DUCHESS! HERE KITTY KITTY!

IT'S NO USE, EDGAR! I MUST HAVE IMAGINED THEY WERE BACK!

I COULD HAVE SWORN I HEARD THE LITTLE ONES MEOWING...

I KNOW THAT MADAME IS VERY UPSET!

NOW... I NEED TO GET OUT THE OLD TRUNK! I HAVE SOMETHING TO SEND TO A VERY DISTANT DESTINATION!

MEANWHILE, IN THE KITCHEN...

TELL ME HIS NAME AGAIN?

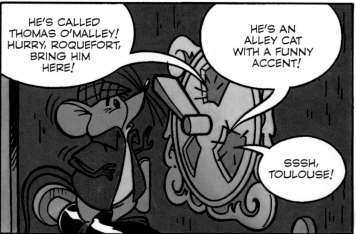

HE'S CALLED THOMAS O'MALLEY! HURRY, ROQUEFORT, BRING HIM HERE!

HE'S AN ALLEY CAT WITH A FUNNY ACCENT!

SSSH, TOULOUSE!

I TOLD YOU IT WAS EDGAR, DIDN'T I?

YES, YOU DID, TOULOUSE!

MISTER... O'MALLEY!

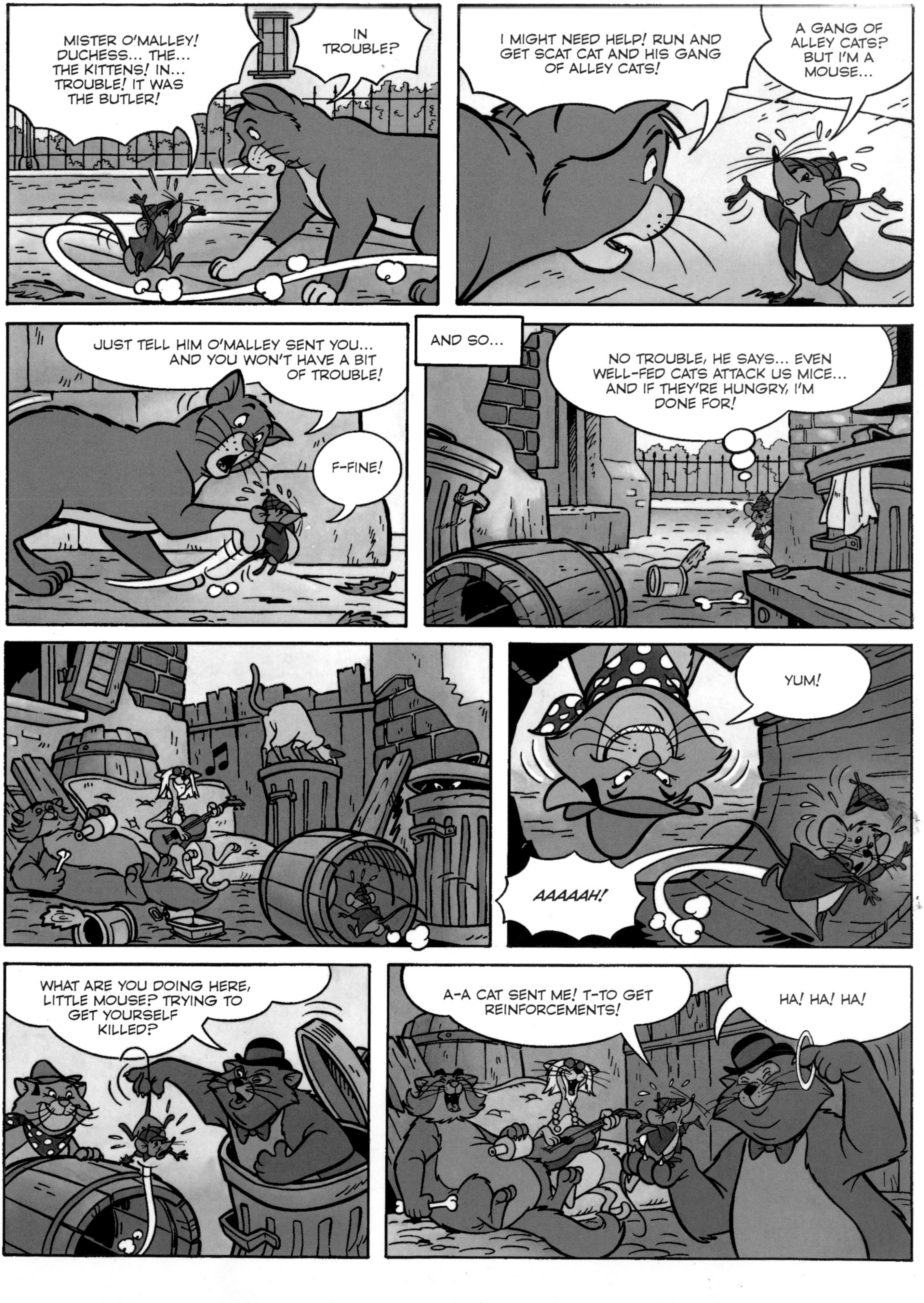
MISTER O'MALLEY! DUCHESS... THE... THE KITTENS! IN... TROUBLE! IT WAS THE BUTLER!
IN TROUBLE?
I MIGHT NEED HELP! RUN AND GET SCAT CAT AND HIS GANG OF ALLEY CATS!
A GANG OF ALLEY CATS? BUT I'M A MOUSE...
JUST TELL HIM O'MALLEY SENT YOU... AND YOU WON'T HAVE A BIT OF TROUBLE!
F-FINE!
AND SO...
NO TROUBLE, HE SAYS... EVEN WELL-FED CATS ATTACK US MICE... AND IF THEY'RE HUNGRY, I'M DONE FOR!
YUM!
AAAAAH!
WHAT ARE YOU DOING HERE, LITTLE MOUSE? TRYING TO GET YOURSELF KILLED?
A-A CAT SENT ME! T-TO GET REINFORCEMENTS!
HA! HA! HA!

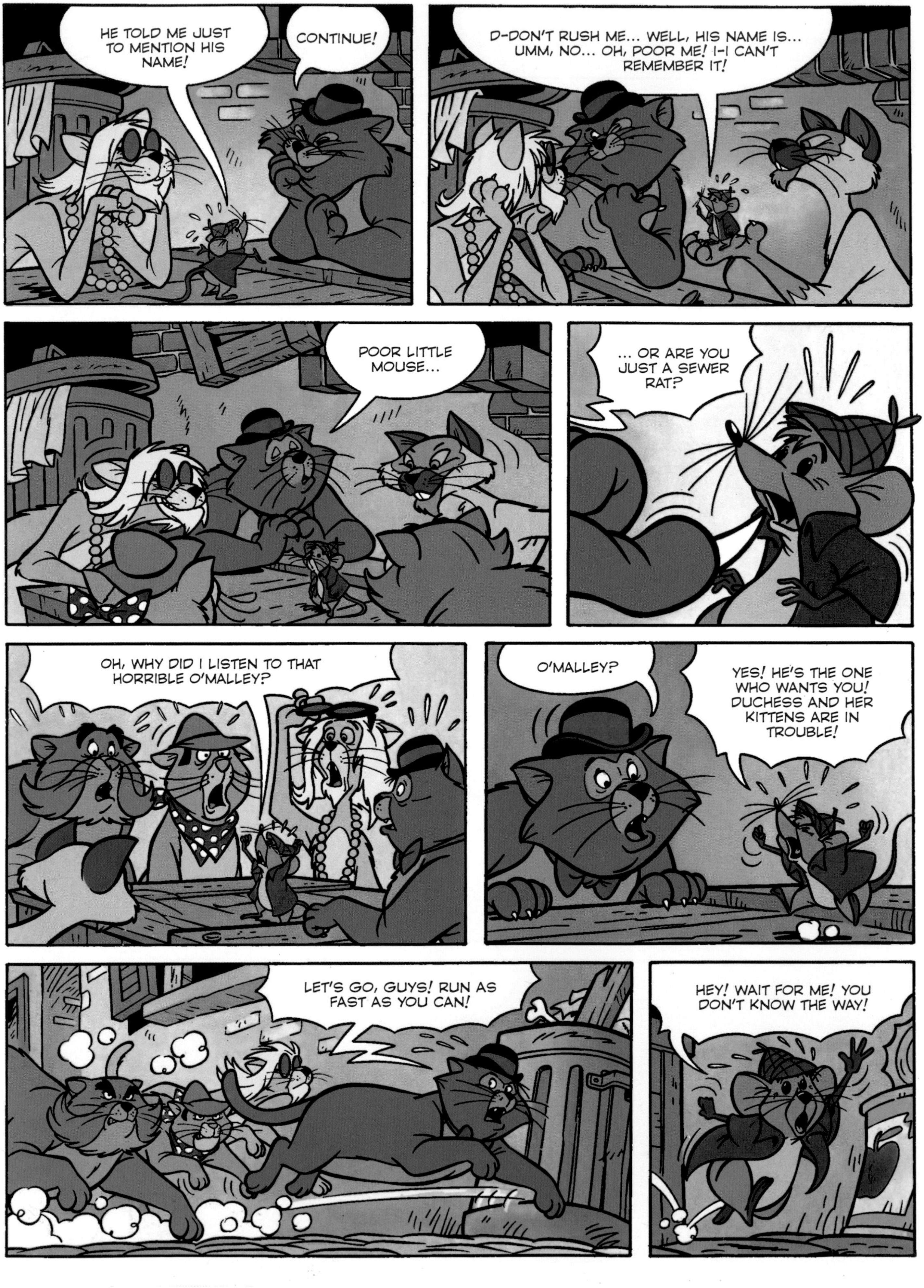
HE TOLD ME JUST TO MENTION HIS NAME!
CONTINUE!
D-DON'T RUSH ME... WELL, HIS NAME IS... UMM, NO... OH, POOR ME! I-I CAN'T REMEMBER IT!
POOR LITTLE MOUSE...
... OR ARE YOU JUST A SEWER RAT?
OH, WHY DID I LISTEN TO THAT HORRIBLE O'MALLEY?
O'MALLEY?
YES! HE'S THE ONE WHO WANTS YOU! DUCHESS AND HER KITTENS ARE IN TROUBLE!
LET'S GO, GUYS! RUN AS FAST AS YOU CAN!
HEY! WAIT FOR ME! YOU DON'T KNOW THE WAY!

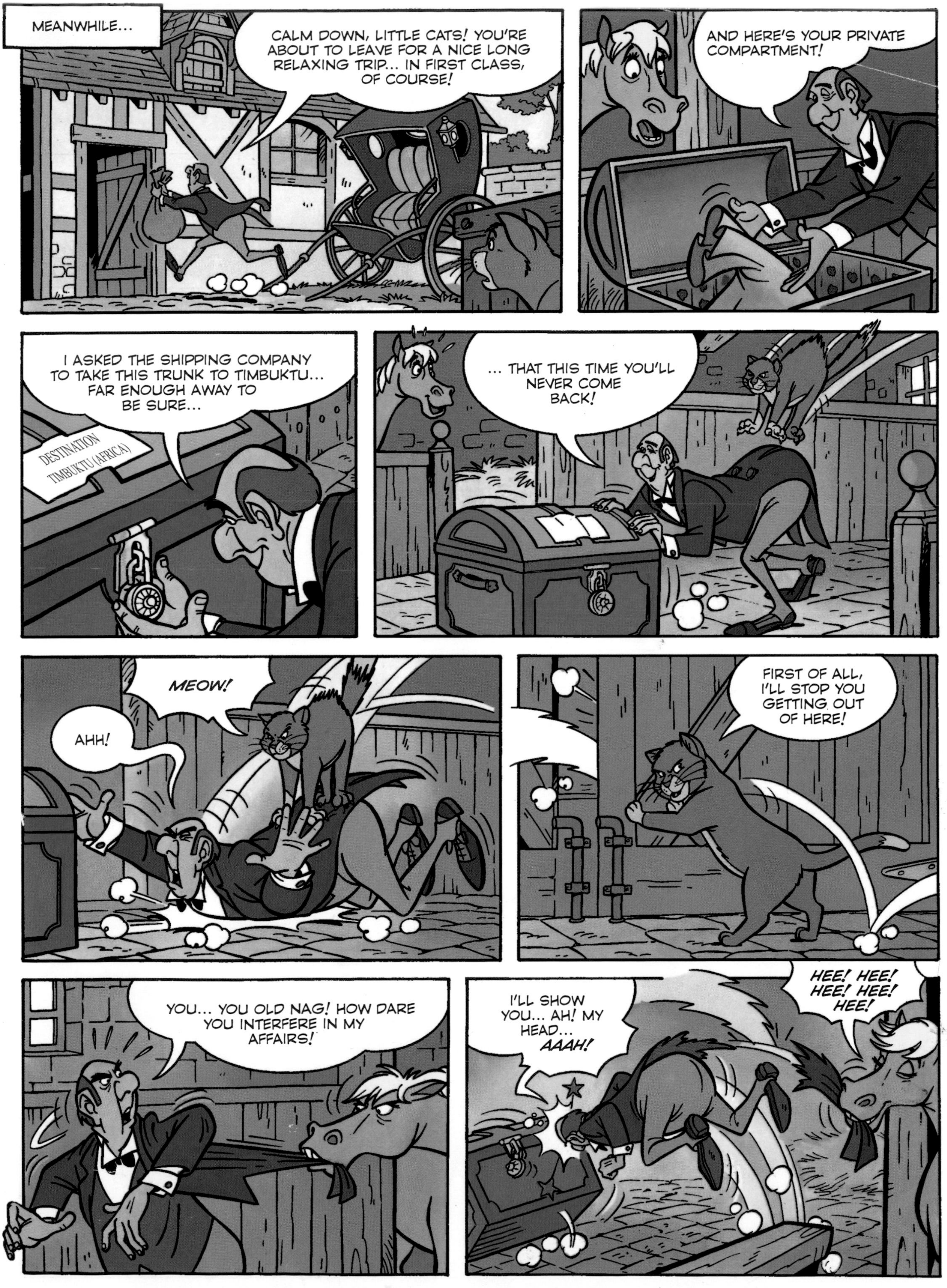
MEANWHILE...
CALM DOWN, LITTLE CATS! YOU'RE ABOUT TO LEAVE FOR A NICE LONG RELAXING TRIP... IN FIRST CLASS, OF COURSE!
AND HERE'S YOUR PRIVATE COMPARTMENT!
I ASKED THE SHIPPING COMPANY TO TAKE THIS TRUNK TO TIMBUKTU... FAR ENOUGH AWAY TO BE SURE...
DESTINATION TIMBUKTU (AFRICA)
... THAT THIS TIME YOU'LL NEVER COME BACK!
MEOW!
AHH!
FIRST OF ALL, I'LL STOP YOU GETTING OUT OF HERE!
YOU... YOU OLD NAG! HOW DARE YOU INTERFERE IN MY AFFAIRS!
I'LL SHOW YOU... AH! MY HEAD... AAAH!
HEE! HEE! HEE! HEE! HEE!

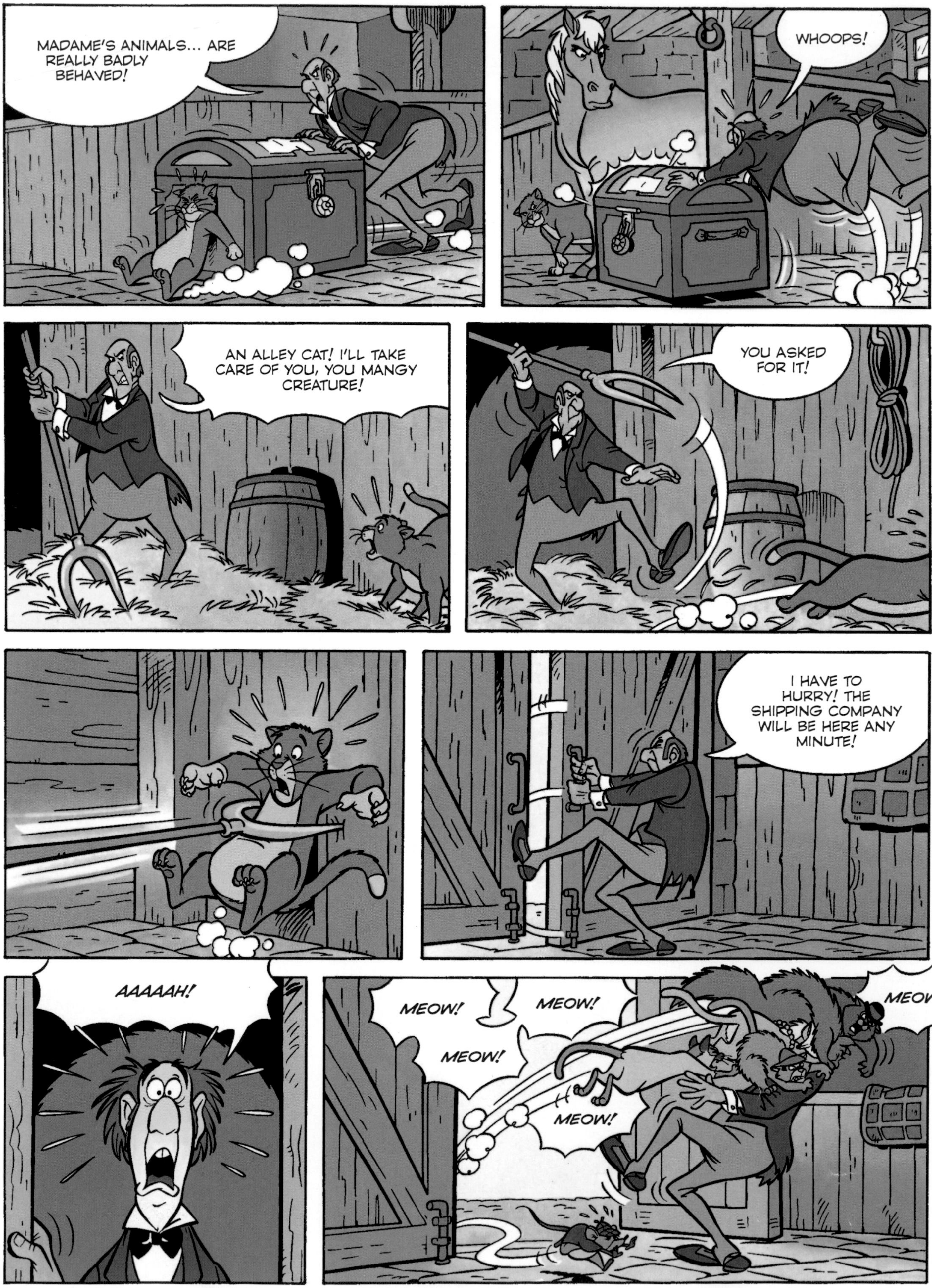
MADAME'S ANIMALS... ARE REALLY BADLY BEHAVED!
WHOOPS!
AN ALLEY CAT! I'LL TAKE CARE OF YOU, YOU MANGY CREATURE!
YOU ASKED FOR IT!
I HAVE TO HURRY! THE SHIPPING COMPANY WILL BE HERE ANY MINUTE!
AAAAAH!
MEOW!
MEOW!
MEOW!
MEOW!
MEOW!

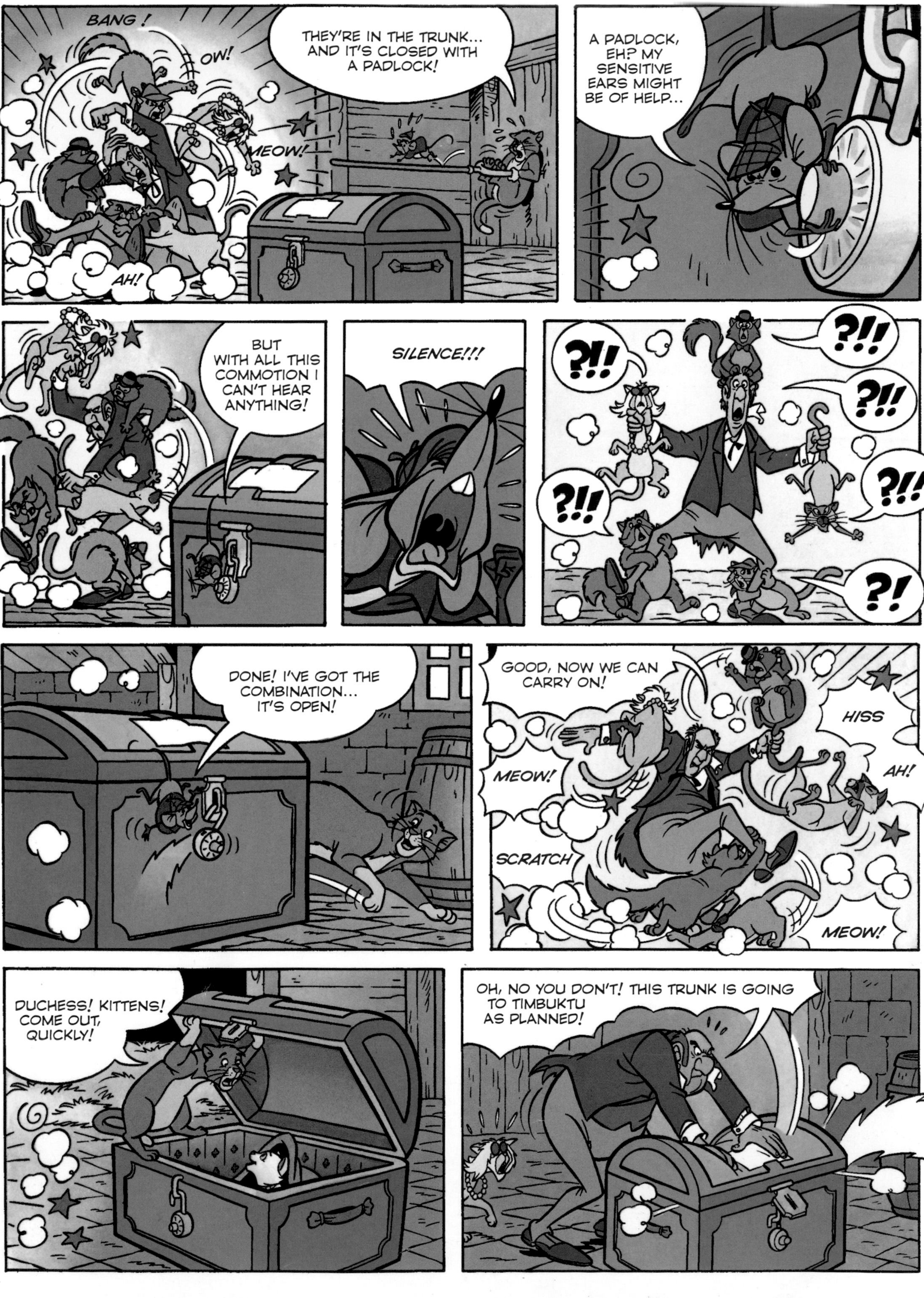
BANG!
OW!
MEOW!
AH!
THEY'RE IN THE TRUNK... AND IT'S CLOSED WITH A PADLOCK!
A PADLOCK, EH? MY SENSITIVE EARS MIGHT BE OF HELP...
BUT WITH ALL THIS COMMOTION I CAN'T HEAR ANYTHING!
SILENCE!!!
?!!
?!!
?!!
?!!
?!!
?!
DONE! I'VE GOT THE COMBINATION... IT'S OPEN!
GOOD, NOW WE CAN CARRY ON!
HISS
AH!
MEOW!
SCRATCH
MEOW!
DUCHESS! KITTENS! COME OUT, QUICKLY!
OH, NO YOU DON'T! THIS TRUNK IS GOING TO TIMBUKTU AS PLANNED!

BUT...

?!

I DON'T THINK SO, MY FRIEND! I THINK THAT THIS WHOLE STORY WILL BE AN IMMENSE CATASTROPHE FOR YOU! HA, HA, HA!

QUICK! LET'S GET OUT!

MEOW!

MEOW!

MEOW!

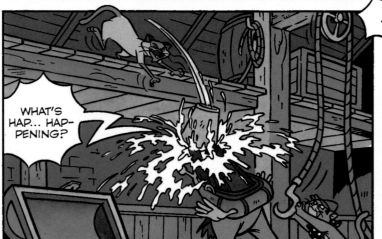

WHAT'S HAP... HAP-PENING?

AAAH!

EVERYONE ON BOARD!

JUST THEN...

THIS MUST BE THE PACKAGE WE'RE SUPPOSED TO PICK UP!

VOILÀ! THIS TRUNK WILL BE IN TIMBUKTU IN A FEW WEEKS!

PFTT! PFTT! PFTT!

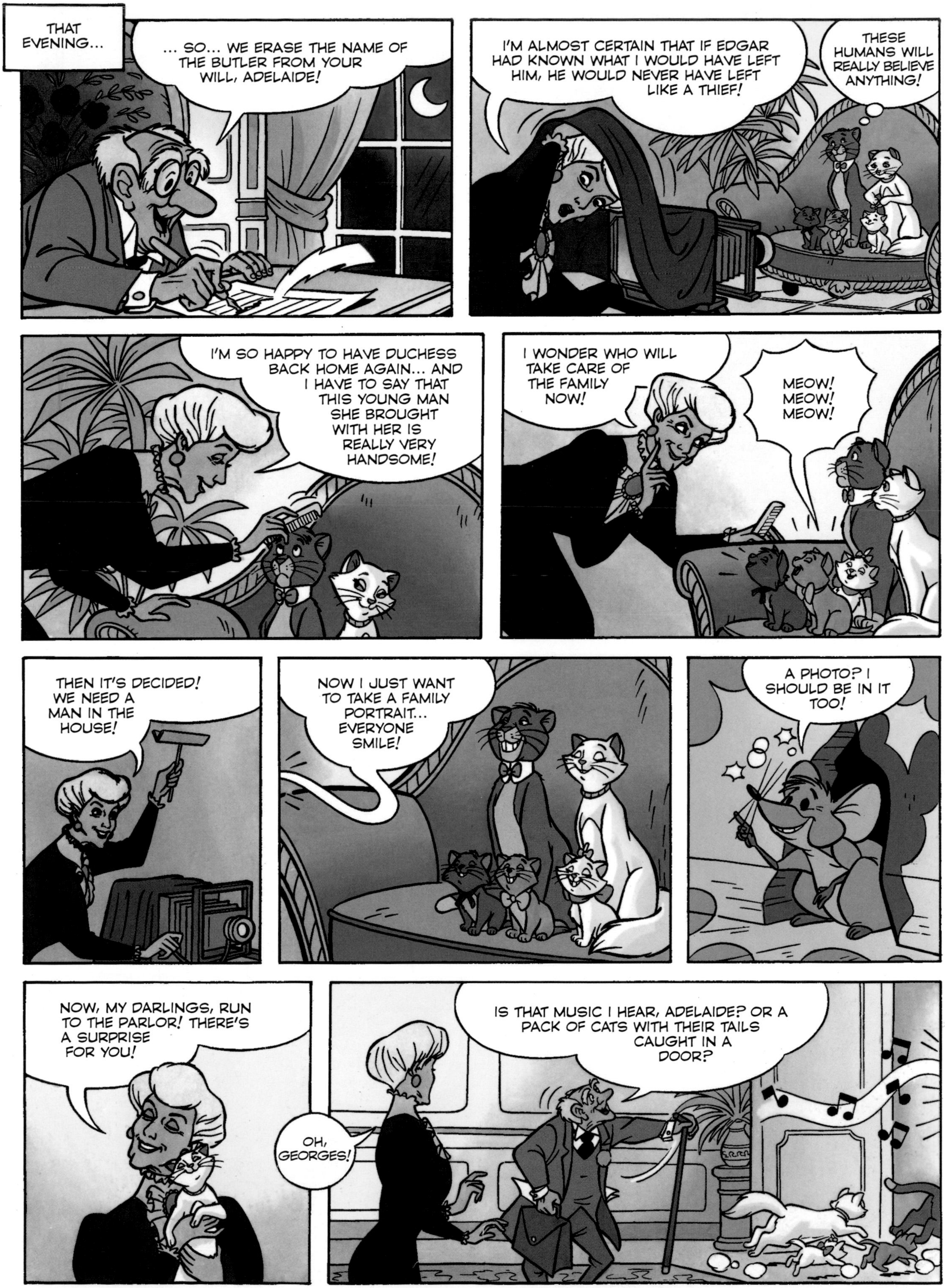
THAT EVENING...
... SO... WE ERASE THE NAME OF THE BUTLER FROM YOUR WILL, ADELAIDE!
I'M ALMOST CERTAIN THAT IF EDGAR HAD KNOWN WHAT I WOULD HAVE LEFT HIM, HE WOULD NEVER HAVE LEFT LIKE A THIEF!
THESE HUMANS WILL REALLY BELIEVE ANYTHING!
I'M SO HAPPY TO HAVE DUCHESS BACK HOME AGAIN... AND I HAVE TO SAY THAT THIS YOUNG MAN SHE BROUGHT WITH HER IS REALLY VERY HANDSOME!
I WONDER WHO WILL TAKE CARE OF THE FAMILY NOW!
MEOW! MEOW! MEOW!
THEN IT'S DECIDED! WE NEED A MAN IN THE HOUSE!
NOW I JUST WANT TO TAKE A FAMILY PORTRAIT... EVERYONE SMILE!
A PHOTO? I SHOULD BE IN IT TOO!
NOW, MY DARLINGS, RUN TO THE PARLOR! THERE'S A SURPRISE FOR YOU!
IS THAT MUSIC I HEAR, ADELAIDE? OR A PACK OF CATS WITH THEIR TAILS CAUGHT IN A DOOR?
OH, GEORGES!

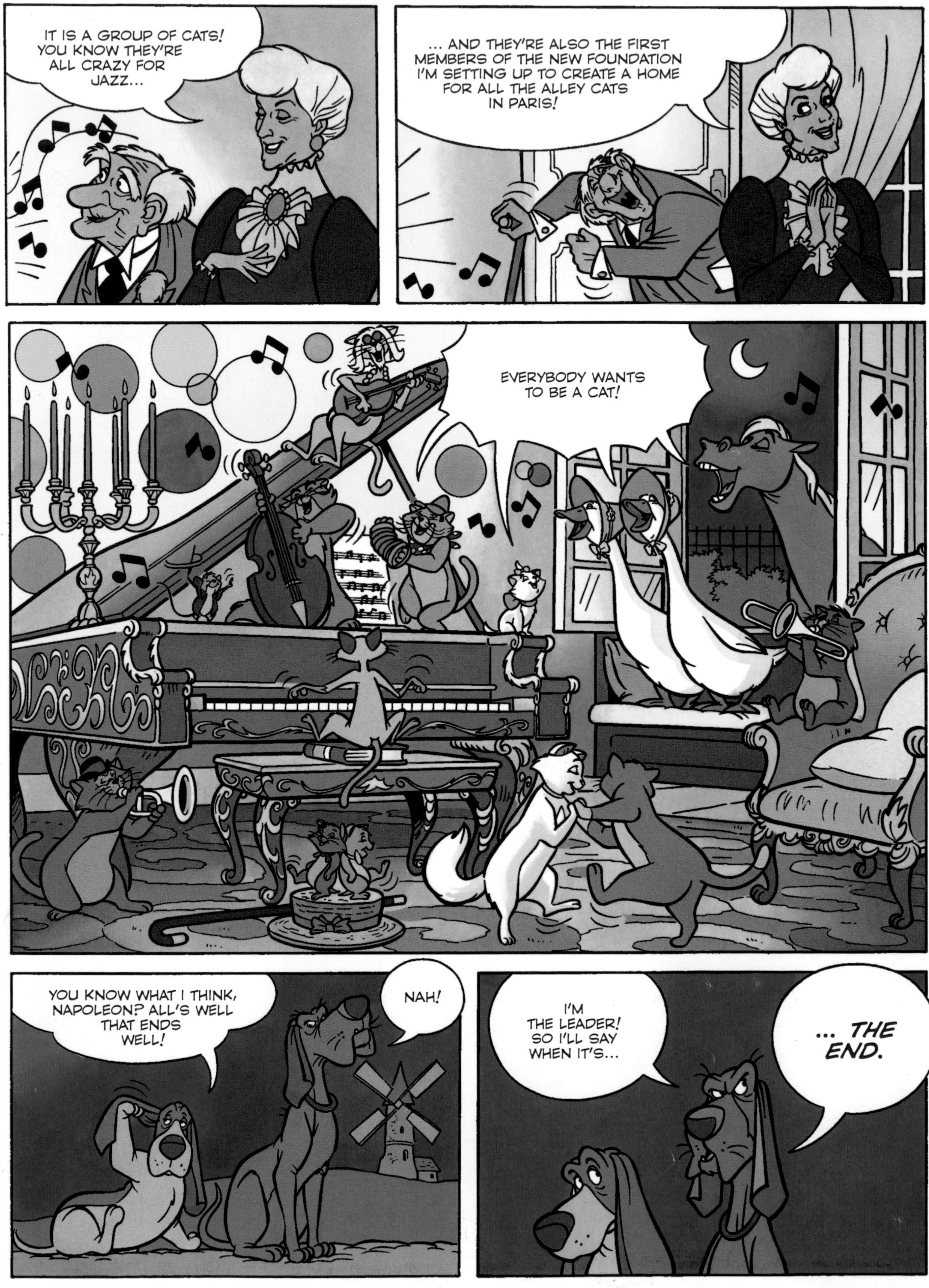
IT IS A GROUP OF CATS! YOU KNOW THEY'RE ALL CRAZY FOR JAZZ...
... AND THEY'RE ALSO THE FIRST MEMBERS OF THE NEW FOUNDATION I'M SETTING UP TO CREATE A HOME FOR ALL THE ALLEY CATS IN PARIS!
EVERYBODY WANTS TO BE A CAT!
YOU KNOW WHAT I THINK, NAPOLEON? ALL'S WELL THAT ENDS WELL!
NAH!
I'M THE LEADER! SO I'LL SAY WHEN IT'S...
... THE END.

DISNEY CLASSICS

COLLECT THEM ALL

Set of 12 Hardcover Books ISBN: 978-1-5321-4531-5

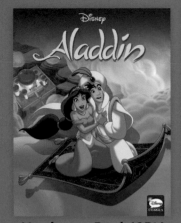

Disney
Aladdin
Hardcover Book ISBN
978-1-5321-4533-9

ALICE
IN
WONDERLAND
Hardcover Book ISBN
978-1-5321-4534-6

THE ARISTOCATS
Hardcover Book ISBN
978-1-5321-4532-2

Disney
Bambi
Hardcover Book ISBN
978-1-5321-4535-3

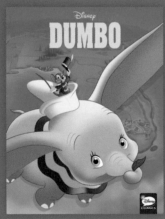

Disney
DUMBO
Hardcover Book ISBN
978-1-5321-4536-0

Disney
THE HUNCHBACK OF NOTRE DAME
Hardcover Book ISBN
978-1-5321-4537-7

Disney
Lady and the TRAMP
Hardcover Book ISBN
978-1-5321-4538-4

Disney
Hardcover Book ISBN
978-1-5321-4539-1

Disney
THE
LION KING
Hardcover Book ISBN
978-1-5321-4540-7

Disney
Peter Pan
Hardcover Book ISBN
978-1-5321-4542-1

Disney
Pinocchio
Hardcover Book ISBN
978-1-5321-4543-8

ROBIN HOOD
REWARD
Hardcover Book ISBN
978-1-5321-4541-4